Radiant

ELIZABETH HAYLEY is actually 'Elizabeth' and 'Hayley', two friends who love reading romance novels to obsessive levels. This mutual love prompted them to put their English degrees to good use by penning their own romances.

BOOK**SHOTS**

STORIES AT THE SPEED OF LIFE

What you are holding in your hands right now is no ordinary book, it's a BookShot.

BookShots are page-turning stories by James Patterson and other writers that can be read in one sitting.

Each and every one is fast-paced, 100% story-driven; a shot of pure entertainment guaranteed to satisfy.

Available as new, compact paperbacks, ebooks and audio, everywhere books are sold.

BookShots – the ultimate form of storytelling. From the ultimate storyteller.

Radiant

The Diamond Trilogy – Part 2

ELIZABETH HAYLEY

1 3 5 7 9 10 8 6 4 2

BookShots
20 Vauxhall Bridge Road
London SW1V 2SA

BookShots is part of the Penguin Random House group of companies
whose addresses can be found at global.penguinrandomhouse.com.

Penguin
Random House
UK

First published by BookShots in 2016

www.penguin.co.uk

A CIP catalogue record for this book is available from the British Library.

ISBN 9781786530486

Printed and bound in Great Britain by Clays Ltd, St Ives Plc

FOREWORD

When I first had the idea for BookShots, I knew that I wanted to include romantic stories. The whole point of BookShots is to give people lightning-fast reads that completely capture them for just a couple of hours in their day—so publishing romance felt right.

I have a lot of respect for romance authors. I took a stab at the genre when I wrote *Suzanne's Diary for Nicholas*. While I was happy with the results, I learned that the process of writing romance novels requires hard work and dedication.

That's why I wanted to pair up with the best romance authors for BookShots. I work with writers who know how to draw emotions out of their characters, all while catapulting their plots forward.

I hope that's why you decided to pick up this book, *Radiant*. Maybe you were so consumed and intrigued by Siobhan and Derick's relationship that you had to read more. Since

Siobhan has moved to Detroit in this book, and Derick doesn't know how to approach her, it might seem as though this couple will never get back together. Unless love really is the most powerful force on earth...

James Patterson

Radiant

Chapter 1

DERICK MILLER MOVED through the space once more, each step on the dark wood floors echoing as he walked. *Pristine white walls, ideal location. It's perfect.*

Janet walked over to where Derick had stopped to look out the window to the street. "Do you have any questions?"

Derick looked over at her and slid a hand into his pocket. "Just one," he said. "How soon can you write up the paperwork? I'll take it."

Chapter 2

SQUEEZING THROUGH THE crowd, Siobhan Dempsey headed toward the back of the large space in the direction of the food.

"You gotta try the dumplings."

Siobhan turned to see Wendell stuffing his face a few feet away. She lifted an amused eyebrow. Ever since she'd moved to Detroit about a month ago and met the happy-go-lucky street artist, Wendell had only talked about two things: food and the building they were currently in.

"I don't gotta to do anything," Siobhan replied with a grin, opting to grab a small sandwich and some fruit instead.

Once he had found out Siobhan wasn't a fan of Chinese food, Wendell had made it his mission to get her to at least try one of the dumplings from a local spot down the block from their apartment building. Between that and attempting to save the building—and, more important, the beautiful mural on its side—from destruction, Wendell had had his hands full. At least he'd been successful at one of his endeavors. "Untrue. You need to celebrate."

"And celebrating means drinking," Lilah slurred as she handed Siobhan a cup of…

"What *is* this?" Siobhan asked, bringing it to her nose and inhaling. She winced when the scent burned her nostrils.

Her roommate leaned in to give Siobhan a nudge, but she lost her balance and nearly fell into the table. "It's moonshine. Jesse's been making it for months. He's gotten pretty good at it the last week or so."

"I don't even know who Jesse is," Siobhan said.

"Woo!" Lilah called loudly as she waved a hand in the air. "Hey, Jesse! Jesse!"

After a moment, a blond-haired guy in a white T-shirt and gray vest gave her a nod and held his drink up.

"That's Jesse," Lilah said.

"Yeah, I got that," Siobhan said with a laugh.

"'Try it," Lilah urged. "It's totes drinkable." Then she nodded dramatically, as if it would strengthen her argument. "You can trust me."

Siobhan narrowed her eyes and tilted her head playfully. "Mmm, why do I feel like that's not true?"

"Listen, Brooklyn," Lilah said, giving Siobhan a bump with her hip. "We took you in and gave you a home. The least you can do is try Jesse's moonshine."

Siobhan laughed at the way Lilah made her sound like a stray kitten. "I'm not really sure how those two things are related to each other, but screw it. We're celebrating, right?" She put the cup up to her lips and drank in long gulps, holding her breath. It did nothing to disguise the flavor.

"Yes!" Lilah yelled. "I knew you had it in you, Brooklyn."

When she couldn't take any more, Siobhan pulled the cup down and shivered. "Jesus, that stuff tastes like rubbing alcohol and shoe polish."

Wendell held out a dumpling to her. "You know what'll cover that taste right up?"

Laughing, Siobhan pushed his hand away. "Get away from me with that."

"Fine," he said. "More for me."

"This is an awesome turnout," Siobhan said. "I had no idea you guys had this many supporters."

"Yeah, I mean, we had thousands of signatures on the petition that circulated around social media, but this is pretty crazy," he said, gesturing to the artists mingling throughout the building.

"So what happened? The city just agreed not to tear it down? I tried to get the story from Lilah, but that's like asking a toddler if they want to go to the zoo. All I got were partial sentences and squeals of delight."

Wendell pulled on the long curly hair on top of his head and laughed. "Someone actually bought it. Thank God there are people who still believe that art is a worthy cause, or this place would be rubble right now."

"Yeah, no kidding. It's nice to finally be in a place that

supports what we're doing. The art community here is amazing." Until Kayla, another artist from New York, had told her about Detroit's art scene, Siobhan hadn't realized how important artists were to the revitalization of the city. But she was happy she'd finally found somewhere that felt like home. "So what's the person going to do with this place?"

Wendell shrugged. "Not sure. But they must have agreed to renovate it into some sort of a usable space, or the city wouldn't have agreed to sell it."

"Yeah, and the buyer definitely has their work cut out for them." She looked around the room at the beat-up walls and concrete floor. But leave it to a bunch of artists to still make it look presentable for a party. The place didn't look half bad, considering its actual condition. Then Siobhan thought of a question she wasn't sure she should ask. But she did anyway. "How do we know the buyer won't paint over the mural when they renovate?"

"The city released a statement saying that stipulation was included in the terms of sale. Gotta love how they tried to save face with that one. They were two seconds from tearing the place down, but a buyer shows up and they refuse to sell until she agrees to keep the mural. Politics—ain't it grand?"

"I'm just happy she let us have the party here and even turned on the electricity for us."

"*She?* You know it's a woman who bought it?"

Wendell grinned broadly. I don't *know*. I'm just hoping. I feel like it's destiny, ya know? Like me and my mystery lady are meant to be together. I can see it now. Art-loving hottie revitalizes city and falls in love with passionate kid from—"

"You're thirty-three."

Wendell looked offended. "You're ruining my fantasy."

"Sorry." Siobhan laughed and waved across the room when she saw her friend Daphne arrive. Like Siobhan, Daphne was an expressionist painter, and she had helped Siobhan get her work into a few of the galleries in the area. Siobhan had even sold two pieces. "I'll talk to you later, okay? Daphne just got here, and I need to talk to her about the exhibit next weekend."

"Okay, okay. I see how it is," Wendell replied with a smile.

Siobhan made her way through the crowd, stopping briefly to chat with a few people she hadn't seen since she'd first gotten to Detroit. She had almost reached Daphne when her phone rang. It was Marnel.

Siobhan hadn't talked to her friend on the phone since she had left New York. They'd texted back and forth a ton and connected through social media, but she hadn't actually spoken to her in more than a month.

"What's up, hooker?" Marnel said when Siobhan answered.

"Hey! It's so good to hear your voice. I miss you." Siobhan moved toward the door and stepped outside so she could talk without yelling over the music.

"We miss you, too," Blaine chimed in. "We're all here. We're just about to leave for the night. Saul hired some girl named Jill as your replacement. She's awful. Constantly dropping stuff and messing up the phone lines." Blaine paused. "Actually, I guess that makes her a lot like you."

"I hate you."

The girls laughed. "But enough about work. What are you up to?" Marnel asked.

"Just standing outside of an abandoned building. You?"

There was silence for a moment before Marnel spoke again. "Siobhan, I know you're struggling, but you need to draw the line somewh—"

"There's a party inside, asshole. I just stepped out so I could hear."

"A party in an abandoned building?" Marnel said. "Why'd you go halfway across the country for the exact same thing you can get in Brooklyn?"

"Stop." Siobhan rolled her eyes. "It's pretty cool, actually." She told the girls about the mural and the building. "The person who bought it let us throw a party here to celebrate. My friend Wendell thinks the buyer is his future wife."

"Sounds like you like it out there," Cory said.

Siobhan smiled and leaned against the wall. "I do. It's been good for me. I've been able to show some of my work and even sold a few paintings. The art community's really welcoming. You guys should come out sometime."

"Yeah, definitely. You should come back here at some point, too," Marnel said. "Maybe for my birthday."

"Yeah, that'd be fun."

"Do you miss it at all?" Cory asked.

Siobhan thought for a moment. "I think I miss the *idea* of New York more than I miss the city itself. The vision I had in my mind before I moved there didn't quite match the reality."

"You mean your dream wasn't to bring menus to the wealthy?" Cory asked.

"Not exactly." The mention of the Stone Room and the people who frequented it brought thoughts into her mind that she'd somehow been able to avoid for the better part of the last month or so.

"So I have to ask," Marnel said. And by the hesitation in her voice, Siobhan knew what was coming next. "Have you heard from him?"

Chapter 3

HEFTING HER BAG higher onto her shoulder, Siobhan waited for the light to turn green so she could cross the busy intersection. As she transferred her weight from one foot to the other, her impatience escalated. She needed to paint.

The phone call from the girls the night before had kick-started an emotional storm of Dust Bowl proportions. Every thought was hidden beneath a thin film of all things Derick.

As she continued walking toward her studio, Siobhan cursed Marnel for approximately the five-hundredth time. She had tried so hard to actively *not* think of Derick over the past month, and it had been working. Perhaps she hadn't been completely happy yet, but she'd been getting there. Making new friends, finding a well-paying job, and having her art be well received had all been major stepping-stones toward an improved mood.

But now she was grumpy. And tense. And…sad. *Damn Marnel.*

Siobhan turned her head to look into her favorite coffee

shop. Since she'd barely slept the night before, she could use some tea to give her some energy. But as she gazed in the window, her heart nearly leaped out of her chest. She jerked to a stop, not because of what she saw *through* the window but because of what she saw reflected *in* it. Or, rather, *who*.

Her sudden stop had caused a man to barrel into her, breaking her focus.

"Sorry," they both muttered as the man proceeded down the sidewalk, and Siobhan's eyes darted back to the window.

He was gone. But she was sure she'd seen…no, it couldn't have been. She hadn't heard from him since she'd left New York. Siobhan shook her head. Now she wasn't just thinking about him, but she was imagining seeing him, too.

Tightening her grip on her bag, she quickened her pace toward her studio, where she could lose herself in her work and forget all about him.

As if it'd be possible to ever forget Derick Miller.

Chapter 4

SIOBHAN SIGHED LOUDLY at the knock on the door. Lilah had texted her a few minutes ago to ask if she was home because she'd forgotten her keys. Again. Siobhan yanked the door open. "I don't think I've ever met a more forgetful—"

The words died in Siobhan's throat. She struggled to find them but could only manage one. And it came out in a whisper. "Derick."

Derick flashed her a small smile. "Hi, Siobhan."

She gripped the door harder in order to keep herself steady. "What are you doing here?"

Thrusting his hands into his pockets, he briefly looked down at the floor before meeting her gaze again, his eyes causing the stir of a familiar warmth that she quickly pushed away. "I wanted to see you."

"Well, you've seen me. Hope it was worth the trip."

"It was."

Siobhan was trying to keep herself detached, distant. But that was pretty damn hard when the man she loved showed up looking like a conglomeration of every fantasy she'd ever had. His gray slacks and white button-down with the collar left open hugged every muscular curve of his body. *Christ.*

She ignored the slight flutter in her chest and the tightening in her core. How dare her body betray her at a time like this? She breathed in deeply, preparing to keep her voice firm. "Listen, Derick, I'm kind of busy. I appreciate that you flew all the way here to see me. I'm not even going to ask how you knew where I lived, because I'm pretty sure I don't want to know the answer. But I don't really have anything to say, so…"

She started to close the door, letting her words trail off because she didn't know how to finish the thought anyway. She'd already said good-bye to Derick. It wasn't an experience she wanted to repeat if she could avoid it.

But before the door closed, Derick's arm shot out and stopped its movement. "You may not have anything to say to me, but I have a lot to say to you. When you left New York, you did it in a verbal blaze of glory. You didn't let me explain things. I need that opportunity, Siobhan. Whether for the chance at fixing things or for closure, I need it. Please."

Siobhan took a deep breath. He was right. She knew he was. She'd gone back to her apartment after their fight, packed up her things, given notice at her jobs, and left New York within a few days. Her transition to her new city had been swift and uncomplicated, despite the deep well of pain she'd refused to acknowledge, and she chose to bury her feelings beneath the foundation of a fresh start.

But talking about Derick, thinking about him, *seeing* him, caused all of that hurt to quake to the surface. She knew that if she didn't deal with it now, her fresh start would crumble around her. "There's a coffeehouse a block away. We can talk there."

Derick's shoulders dropped in what Siobhan could only guess was relief. He backed away from the door and motioned down the hall with his hand. "After you."

Chapter 5

HOLDING THE TEA she'd ordered, Siobhan slid into the seat across from Derick. She glanced out the window, squinting at the afternoon sun. "So what is it you need to say?"

Derick cleared his throat, trying like hell to remember what he'd wanted to tell her since that day in his apartment. He'd practiced it a thousand times on the flight here, although the last thing he wanted was for it to seem rehearsed. It probably was a good thing that right now, he couldn't think of anything other than the way Siobhan's blue eyes sparkled in the sunlight. Somehow they looked clearer than they ever had.

"I believed in you, Siobhan," Derick began. "I still do. But at some point, you stopped believing in yourself. And I didn't want you to lose hope. That's why I bought your paintings. I was trying to buy you time so you could keep pursuing your dream." The words came out much faster than he'd meant for them to, and they weren't the ones he'd prepared.

Siobhan lowered her gaze. "You tainted it."

"What?"

She raised her head slowly again, her eyes locking with his. "My dream. The excitement that comes with having sold my first painting…I'll never get that back. I know that because when I sold my first one here, I didn't feel much of anything."

Derick's face fell. "I didn't mean for that to happen. You were upset, and I thought I had the power to fix it. So I did. Or I tried to."

Siobhan sat back, tucking her hair behind her ear and then folding her arms across her chest. "Do you want to know what I wished for that day?" she asked.

"What day?" Derick's voice was low. Soft.

"That day at the Empire State Building." She didn't wait for him to answer. "I wished I could start making a career out of something I love."

Derick averted his gaze out the window before forcing it back to her. She looked nearly as hurt as the last time he'd seen her.

"That wish came true. Too bad it cost me way more than a penny."

Derick sighed heavily. "I'm so sorry, Siobhan. I need you to know that."

Her eyes narrowed. "That's why you flew five hundred miles? To tell me you're sorry?"

"No." His voice was calm, but there was a firmness to it. "I flew five hundred miles because even though I told you that one day you'd run and I wouldn't come after you, that isn't true. It'll never be true, Siobhan. Not when you love someone the way I love you."

She inhaled a shaky breath but didn't say anything.

"No relationship's perfect. You have to know that. Not ours. Not anyone's." One corner of his lip turned up into a small smile. "But we're great together, and I think you know that, too." He paused, giving her time to take in his words. "So give me one more chance. Please. Give *us* one more chance."

"Derick, I—"

He reached across the table and gave her hand a gentle squeeze. She didn't pull away from him. That was something. "I don't want an answer right now. I don't deserve one. Just think about what I've said."

Then he slid a card across the table to her. "This is where I'm staying. I'll be here through Tuesday. Promise you'll think about it?"

She glanced at the card quickly before shoving it into her purse and looking back to him. "Okay," she said quietly. "I'll think about it."

Chapter 6

PAINTING. IT WAS the only thing Siobhan was becoming *more* sure of as she sat in her small studio and allowed her emotions to pour onto her canvas. One didn't have to be Freud to figure out that the deep blues and purples her muse was preferring today were in direct relation to the dour mood she was in.

The looming buildings she was painting could have been from any city. There were no defining characteristics, and even she didn't know if she was depicting Detroit or New York. Maybe neither. Maybe both. She realized that she didn't know either city well enough to render an accurate drawing of any of its well-known buildings.

And that was the real crux of the problem. How was she supposed to know where she belonged when she didn't let herself get completely attached to any place? She had always known what she wanted, but she was at a complete loss as to where she would find it.

It was all like a jumbled-up science experiment. Art was

the control, the only constant in her life. She had hypothe-sized that her career would thrive in New York, but she'd been wrong. So she'd had to adapt and change the climate to one that would encourage her talent to grow. What she hadn't anticipated—what she supposed no one ever anticipated—was the variable. And her variable was Derick.

She stood and looked out of her studio window. She liked what she saw—liked this city much better than the one she'd left. The hustle and bustle below her was hurried yet less fran-tic than the traffic she had endured for five months. Or maybe it was just the new Siobhan who was less frantic.

What sat in front of her was a future. There was no room for the past in what she was creating in Detroit. Especially when that past was tumultuous and painful.

Quickly rinsing her brushes and putting away her supplies, Siobhan hardened her resolve. She grabbed her purse and hur-ried down to the street to hail a cab. She didn't need the card Derick had given her to know where to tell the driver to go. She'd looked at it enough over the thirty or so hours since he'd given it to her. "MGM Grand Detroit, please."

The man pulled out into traffic, and Siobhan practiced her speech during the drive. She had to be calm but firm. Derick had to understand that she meant what she was saying, and the only way to make sure of that was to be unaffected and confident. So as she rode up in the elevator to Derick's floor, she told herself that she'd go inside, sit him down, and ratio-nally explain how she felt.

Holding her head high and shifting her shoulders back, she knocked on the door. Derick opened it almost immediately, and the sight of him in dark-rinsed jeans and a tight white T-shirt caused a rush of fury to flood through her. How dare he always look so fucking perfect when she was a goddamn mess?

And then he had the audacity to smile that dazzling smile that always left her a little breathless. Or at least it used to, before she'd decided she hated him—which she had just done in that very moment.

"I need you to leave and never come back," she said.

That hadn't been at all what she'd practiced, but it still captured the gist of what she was going for. And it had the added bonus of wiping that smile off his face.

However, as it turned out, she preferred the infuriating smile to the crestfallen look that replaced it. Siobhan had never been a mean person, at least not on purpose. And hurting Derick made her chest ache in a way she had never felt before. She sighed and relaxed her rigid posture. "Can I come in?"

Derick nodded and stepped back from the door.

Siobhan walked into the living room and then turned to look at him. "I meant what I said, even if I wish I'd said it differently. This is a fresh start for me. I can't bring old drama into a new opportunity. It's not fair to me, and it isn't fair to you, either. Because no matter how much I'd try to hide it, if things failed out here, I'd blame you for it."

Derick's brow furrowed. "How would your failure be my

fault? Especially since all I've ever wanted was for you to succeed?"

"I didn't say it would be your fault. I said I'd blame you for it."

"But how does that make any sense?"

"Because I already blame you for New York. It's not your *fault* I wasn't successful there. Logically I know that I didn't give my art the time and energy it needed. But the emotional side of me blames you for it. Because you were the reason I didn't have more time and energy. And you were also the reason I had to leave." She sighed heavily. "But the truth is, even before you came into my life, I didn't have enough time to devote to my art. Bills and rent took priority."

Derick plopped down on the couch and rubbed his hands over his face. He looked up at Siobhan with clear frustration. "But that's what I was trying to give you: time. I thought that if you sold your paintings, you'd be able to devote more time to your art because you wouldn't have to work so hard."

Siobhan sat in a chair across from him. "When your app first took off, did you have to work hard to keep it going?"

"Of course."

Siobhan widened her eyes, willing him to see her point.

He waved a hand at her. "That's not the same thing. I was working hard on my business. You were working hard on about four different businesses, and none of them was your passion."

"But it was still hard work," Siobhan said, her voice getting louder. "I would've been able to look back on it in ten years and say I did everything I could to make myself successful. I would've been proud of the journey, even if I didn't end up where I hoped I would. But then you swooped in and paved my path in gold when I never asked you to."

"So you're mad at me because I stole your chance to call yourself a starving artist? Sorry to ruin your street cred, Siobhan." Derick stood and stalked toward her.

"God, you're really such an asshole."

"I'm also clearly a masochist. Because despite your rejecting me at every turn, I can't let you go. Do you want to know why that is?"

"Not really," she muttered, even though she definitely wanted to know.

He continued as if she hadn't said anything. "Because even though I have everything any reasonable man could want, I'm not content with it. And I never will be, because the one thing I don't have is you." He paused for a moment, letting his stare hold hers. "You're the only thing I'll ever want, Siobhan."

The words hit Siobhan square in the chest, but her pride wouldn't let her show it. "I never asked you to want me."

"No shit. You've never asked me for anything. God forbid you should accept help from anyone, even though you desperately need it."

She stepped into his personal space. The anger radiating off both of them was incendiary. "The only thing I need is for you to leave."

He bent down slightly so his eyes could burn into hers. "What about what I need?"

Those words were like a bucket of ice-cold water and caused her to jerk back a few steps. As Siobhan processed them, she realized how true they were. Even though Derick's actions had been misguided, he'd only ever had her in mind when he did them. But what had she ever done for him?

Even after realizing this, her stubbornness wouldn't allow her to tell him what he needed to hear. "What do you want me to say, Derick? That you deserve better?" It hurt her to say the words. Because even though they'd been said sarcastically, there was some truth in them.

And as she watched a change come over Derick's face, she understood that he knew she meant them. He closed the distance between them. "God, how can you still not get it?" Putting a thumb under her chin, he tilted her head up so she was forced to look at him. "There *is* no better than you."

And before she could respond, his lips were on hers.

Chapter 7

SIOBHAN WASN'T GIVING IN. She wasn't. But he was so warm, and his kiss was so intoxicating, and his scent was so familiar that she couldn't pull away, even though her brain was yelling at her in warning.

"Siobhan…" he murmured as he nipped her earlobe. "You know you want to."

"You have no idea what I want."

He hoisted her up and walked her over to the nearest wall, which he pressed her against as he continued his assault with his mouth. "I think I know *exactly* what you want."

She was not proud of the moan that escaped her or of the way her legs were wrapped like a vise around his hips.

"See?" he said, and she could feel his smile against her neck.

"God, of all the hot men in New York, why did I have to fall in love with the most annoying one?"

Suddenly, those words, which she hadn't meant to say, brought Derick to a screeching halt.

"Why are you stopping? I told you that you didn't know what I wanted."

She began pushing against his chest, but he kept her pinned against the wall with his hips as he grabbed her wrists with his hands and pinned them, too. "Stop pushing me away, and say that again."

Siobhan jutted out her chin. "You don't know what I want."

His grip on her wrists tightened, not to the point of pain but to make it clear that he meant business. "This is your opportunity to give me what I need, Siobhan. Please. Give it to me."

She wanted to keep fighting with him. She wanted to get down and walk out of that hotel room and never think about Derick Miller again. But that was never going to happen. Because as she stared into his light-brown eyes, she knew that she'd think of him every day, just as she'd thought about him every day since she'd left him, even though she hadn't let herself admit it.

Derick Miller hadn't just tainted her art, he'd tainted her happiness. It was now completely and utterly dependent on her being with him. She'd been a fool to think differently.

She pulled her arms down, hoping Derick would release them. He did. Placing her hands on his cheeks, she gazed deeply into his eyes. "I love you, Derick. And despite the fact that you're completely infuriating, I probably always will."

He slid his arms around her waist and held her tight. "I love you, too. And I'll never stop."

She rolled her eyes and said, "I know."

"I'm glad we've made that clear," he said. And then his mouth was back on hers. There was no pretty way to describe what he was doing. He was devouring her.

His hands slid down to squeeze her ass and pull her toward his erection.

She groaned at the feel of him. "Too many clothes."

He put her down long enough for them to rip the clothes off each other. Then he hoisted her back up and slammed her against the wall.

Sliding her hand into his thick hair, she pulled on the strands as he bit and sucked on her neck.

This wasn't going to be gentle makeup sex. This was going to be a savage reclaiming.

Her free hand scratched down his back as the steady grind of his hips pressed her spine into the wall. They'd both be wearing each other's marks the next day.

She shifted up so she could slide herself down on his rock-hard cock. He buried his face in the crook of her neck as she seated herself on him fully. Their skin was damp and hot as they breathed together for a moment before Derick dipped his knees and then thrust up into her.

He buried his cock deep into her before retreating and repeating. Her breasts bounced with the movement, causing her nipples to graze the hair on his pecs, making the oversensitized buds zing with ecstasy.

Moans and gasps filled the room, and Derick pumped

wildly into her. She wasn't going to last much longer. She'd missed this too much. Missed *him* too much.

"Oh, Derick, I can't...you're going to make me come."

His breath was hot on her ear as he said, "Do it. Come all over my cock."

The words were probably the hottest she'd ever had said to her, and they caused her orgasm to hit her suddenly. The pleasure seemed to be coming from everywhere: her neck as Derick sucked on her skin, her nipples as they rubbed deliciously against him, and her clit as it pulsed when Derick's cock thrust deeply into her.

Her entire body was taut with her release, quaking with satisfaction. She kissed him everywhere she could reach, as he continued to pump into her. "Yes. Feels so good. Want you inside me, Derick. I never want you anywhere else."

His hips bucked a few more times before his rhythm became erratic. Thrusting hard one last time, he came inside her. He continued moving, letting his cock empty completely before he pulled back enough for them to get some cool air on their skin.

They kissed lazily for a few minutes as they slowly let their bodies come down from the high they'd just experienced. Finally, Derick stopped kissing her long enough to look into her eyes. "Does this mean you forgive me?"

Siobhan smiled. "I may need more convincing," she said as she pulled his lips back to hers.

Chapter 8

SLIDING AN ARM around Siobhan's body, Derick let himself feel the gentle rise and fall of her chest as she slept peacefully beside him. God, he'd missed her.

He opened his eyes and smiled as they settled on her. The look on her face was relaxed, content. And for the first time in more than a month, he felt that way, too.

His gaze drifted farther down, taking in the smooth skin on her chest. He moved his hand up to run his thumb over a few red marks he'd put there the night before. A part of him hoped he wouldn't wake her. But another part—which was currently hard and pressing against Siobhan's warm thigh—had different plans.

"I love you," he said softly in her ear as he trailed kisses down her neck to her breasts. From the moment he had first seen her in the Stone Room, he'd known he would never get enough of her. Although she'd been the one to trip, it was Derick who had fallen.

Eventually, she began to stir, although he suspected she'd actually been awake longer than she let on. "I love you, too," she said.

Derick looked up to see her eyes still closed and a smile on her face. "Say that again." He'd given the same directive last night, but he couldn't help it. He didn't think he'd ever grow tired of hearing it.

This time she opened her eyes and brought a hand down to tangle in his hair as he slowly moved up her body to hover directly above her. "I love you, Derick. I meant it when I said it last night."

"I know you did. I just like the sound of it."

She gave him a slow, innocent kiss on his lips. "You do, do you?"

Derick nodded and leaned in to nibble just below her ear. "Yup. You know what else I like the sound of?"

"What's that?"

"You coming underneath me," he rasped. "Or on top of me. Or in front of me. I'm not picky."

Siobhan giggled. Whether it was at his words or what he was doing to her neck, he wasn't sure.

"God, I've missed you."

Siobhan wrapped her arms around his neck as he pulled back to stare at her. "Derick?"

"Yeah?"

"Stop talking, and make love to me."

Knowing the effect he had on her, Derick grinned wider.

Then he leaned down until his lips made contact with her soft, pink ones and kissed the hell out of her.

His tongue moved against hers hungrily, and his teeth nipped at her bottom lip every so often. She moaned softly below him, but the noises she made grew louder and wilder as Derick's kisses landed on her jaw and collarbone.

His cock was unbelievably hard, making him groan as he ground against her. Then he moved lower, paying special attention to her nipples and the smooth, pale skin of her breasts. He thought about what it would be like to come on them, to kneel over her with his cock in his hand and bring himself to release while she watched him.

Finally, he brought his face lower, nipping at her stomach and tracing a wet line with his tongue down her abdomen.

Siobhan arched below him. "God, Derick. Keep going."

His hand slid lightly down the outside of her thigh, and he glanced up at her. Her cheeks were flushed with desire. "I didn't exactly have any plans of stopping."

Siobhan didn't speak, instead opting to guide his head lower until his lips met the wetness between her thighs. He'd even missed the taste of her—how slippery and sweet she was on his mouth. He could get lost in her.

She writhed with every stroke of his tongue, until she begged to have his cock inside her. Instead, he glided two fingers into her slowly, using his thumb to work the sensitive nerve endings of her clit while his fingers massaged the insides of her. God, she was warm and wet and ready.

Kissing her thigh as he draped it over his shoulder to move his lips down to her knee, he listened to her moans and shaky breaths as he continued to bring her slowly to the release he could tell was imminent. "Let go," he said, when he could tell she was barely hanging on.

She rode his hand for a few more moments before her body tensed around his fingers and she bucked against him, reaching behind her to squeeze the pillow. "Jesus, Derick." She panted as her movements slowed.

When Derick knew she was done, he removed his fingers slowly, licking them as he stalked slowly up her body. Her eyes were closed, and she looked thoroughly satisfied. "Did that feel good?" he asked.

Siobhan nodded, contentment clear on her face.

"Good," he said. "Because I'm going to make you do it again."

Siobhan's eyes opened, her gaze heated as she stared at him silently. She licked her lips before her teeth settled on the bottom one to bite it. God, she was sexy.

Her lips parted to let his tongue enter, and she wrapped her thighs around him. She was slick against his shaft as she rubbed herself over him. He wouldn't be able to hold off much longer if she kept this up, but he wanted to get her close again before he buried himself inside her.

Heavy moans and gasps of pleasure filled the room, and Siobhan let a few soft curses escape her as she ground against him. A few moments later, she reached between them to grab his cock in her hand. He wasn't going to last long.

"I need this," she said.

And that's all it took. In an instant, Derick was plunging so deeply inside her that there was no space at all between them. And he wanted it to stay that way.

They found their rhythm easily, a slow grind that gradually increased its speed. Last night had been so frantic, so full of raw emotion. This time was like a practiced dance, two bodies linked together as they moved as one.

Derick thrust sharply as she moaned beneath him, her heartbeat strong against his chest as his hand kneaded her scalp. He couldn't hold off much longer, and he hoped Siobhan felt the same. "God, baby…I can't…You have to…"

"Almost, Derick," she said on an exhalation.

His movements got more aggressive as he pulled out nearly completely and then buried himself back inside her until his pelvis rubbed the spot he knew would make her come undone.

And she did.

Her back arched as she clenched around him, her body quaking with release. As soon as Derick knew she was coming, so was he. He nearly shook with the orgasm he'd been holding back since he'd woken up next to her.

When they'd both come down from their sexual high, Siobhan ran a hand through his hair and along his beard to caress the side of his face. "So how is this going to work?" she asked softly.

Chapter 9

HE FIGURED THIS was a conversation best had on a full stomach, so he ordered breakfast.

Siobhan put some butter on her toast and then looked up at him. "So what are you thinking?"

"That you look hot in my T-shirt." It was true, though it obviously didn't answer the question she'd really been asking.

She ripped off a piece of crust and tossed it across the small table at him. "Stop stalling. This is something we need to discuss."

Derick knew she had a point. But he also knew that this conversation wouldn't be as easy as the last twelve hours had been. "I want you to move back to New York."

Siobhan's eyes widened. "I just moved here, and things are going well for me. You can't be serious."

"I am."

Siobhan put her toast down and leaned against the back of the chair. "Derick, be reasonable."

"I think it *is* reasonable. If your art career is going well in

Detroit, I see no reason why that success can't continue in New York. It's the city you always dreamed of living in anyway, right?"

"Yeah. But you can't expect me to pick up and move right now."

"I didn't say I wanted you to move *now*. I mean, I *do* want you to move now, but logically I know that's unfair." Derick took a sip of his coffee. "And more than that, I know you'd never agree to it."

Siobhan seemed to relax a little at his words, but she still looked uncertain.

"I'm more than willing to fly back and forth as much as my schedule will allow for the next few months. It'll give your art more time to take off, and it'll give us time to…get reacquainted."

"Why do I think *get reacquainted* means have lots of sex?"

Derick smirked as he gave her a heated gaze. "Because you're a dirty girl."

Siobhan gave him a playful kick to the shin under the table.

"I'm being serious, though. I know you need to see where our relationship's going before you commit to something as big as moving back to New York. So let's see how things go. If things are working out between us, I'd like you to consider moving back." He leaned forward in his chair to take her hand in his. "What do you say?"

Siobhan looked at him, a slight glimmer in her eye. "I say you'd better be on your best behavior, Mr. Miller."

Chapter 10

IN THE TWO days after Siobhan and Derick changed their relationship status to "on again" and Derick decided to extend his stay by a week, they hadn't spent much time out of bed. But Siobhan already knew they got along well sexually. If they were going to try to make a go of things, they needed to spend their time doing activities that required clothing.

She walked over to the bed and smacked Derick's bare ass. "Get up." He didn't move a muscle. "God, how did you ever found a billion-dollar business when you can't even be bothered to sit upright?" She smirked as she leaned down to smack him again. "Let's go, Roderick."

Quick as lightning, he turned and grabbed her hand before it made contact with his skin, causing her to sprawl next to him on the bed. "Don't call me that."

She looked at him curiously. "It's your name, isn't it?"

"It's not one I go by anymore."

"Why not?"

Derick scrubbed a hand over his face and sighed. "Because

it was my father's middle name. When he left, I didn't want any part of myself associated with him, including my name. So I had my mom and my brother start calling me Derick instead."

"I'm sorry. I never knew."

"It's fine," Derick assured her as he placed a hand on her. "It doesn't matter."

"It matters to me. I should've let you explain a long time ago," she said. "It's your name. It's who you are."

"It's not who I am anymore." And with that, Derick wrapped his arms around her and pulled her close. "The only thing that matters is that we're here together now. Let's just let the past stay in the past."

"Okay," she answered quietly.

"Now," he said, a previously absent smile lighting up his face. "Less talking, more nudity." He let a hand drift down and pull up her shirt, though he stopped at her ribs and dug his fingers in.

Siobhan began laughing as she tried to escape his grasp. "Stop. Stop!"

"Tell me you love me." She could feel his smile against the back of her neck.

"No." He dug his fingers in again, causing an unladylike snort to leave her as she gasped for breath through her laughter.

He flipped her onto her back so he could perform his tickle assault with both hands. "Just say it. You know you want to."

She bucked and thrashed as she tried to dislodge his muscular body from where it straddled her hips. "You'd better not fall asleep tonight, Miller."

Pinning her hands to the bed, he leaned in close. "And why would that be?" His smile was smug, which would have infuriated her if he wasn't so damn gorgeous.

"Because I'm going to exact my revenge as soon as your eyes close."

He quirked his lips to one side as though he were pondering her words. Then he looked down and smirked. "I'm not worried."

He resumed his tickling until she yelled out, "Okay, okay, I'll say it!"

As soon as he released her, she narrowed her eyes at him. She contemplated continuing to be difficult, but as she took in the wide smile on his face and the light in his eyes, she found herself wanting to say the words. She brought her hands up to his cheeks, pulled him down, and kissed him. "I love you."

He pulled back and gazed at her for a bit. He pecked one more kiss to her lips and said, "See? That wasn't so hard, was it?" Then he leaped off the bed.

She watched him grab a pair of boxers and head for the bathroom. "I still may kill you," she muttered.

"I'll keep it in mind," he replied, the lightness in his voice making it clear that he wasn't concerned. He walked into the bathroom but poked his head out just before he shut the door. "Siobhan?"

She let her head flop to the right so she could look at him.

"I love you, too," he said, before shutting the door and taking a shower.

Siobhan got off the bed, straightened out her clothes, and fixed her hair in the mirror while she waited for Derick. Once he was finally ready, he called for a car that would be there within fifteen minutes. As they made their way down to the lobby, Derick asked where they were going.

"Belle Isle," Siobhan informed him.

"What's that?"

"Honestly, I don't really know. I've heard it mentioned a bunch since I got here, but I've never been there."

Derick grabbed her hand and interlocked their fingers. "So we're going to explore a new place together?"

Siobhan smiled at him. "Yup."

"Awesome." Derick led her out to the black SUV that was waiting for them, slipping his Aviators on as soon as they got outside.

He told the driver their destination, and they were off. Siobhan pointed out the limited number of landmarks she could remember. When they passed the warehouse with the mural that her friends had fought to save, Siobhan told Derick the story about it.

"Your friends sound like good people. I'm glad it worked out for them."

"Me, too."

They arrived at Belle Isle, an island park on the Detroit River.

"It's really beautiful here," Derick said.

"I know. I'm glad we came."

Derick bumped her shoulder with his. "Well, I'm always glad when that happens."

Siobhan laughed and bumped him back. "You're so immature."

"All part of my charm."

Since she couldn't disagree, she stayed quiet.

They hiked the trails around the island before deciding to head toward the Nature Zoo.

"That's weird," Derick mumbled as he looked at the map they'd picked up when they first arrived.

"What is?"

"This says we're *at* the zoo." Derick looked around. "But that can't be right."

Siobhan scanned the area before tapping Derick on the bicep and pointing. "There's a deer."

Derick looked in the direction she indicated. "What?"

"Right there. There's a deer."

Derick looked from the deer to the map and back to the deer. "That can't be all there is."

"I think I see a sign for turtles over there."

Squinting to see the sign, Derick sighed before turning toward Siobhan. They looked at each other for a moment before they both broke into laughter.

Swinging his arms around, Derick gestured around them. "This is *not* a zoo," he said, somewhat breathless from laughter. "The brochure is false advertising."

That made Siobhan start laughing all over again. These were the carefree moments she loved. The times when the two of them got out of their own way and just enjoyed life together.

"I'm sorry I made us walk over here. This is a total disappointment." Derick put his arm around her shoulders, his fingers gently tracing soft patterns on her arm.

"Nah, it was an adventure," she assured him. "It's a great story we'll be able to tell people. The time we went to the zoo that really wasn't."

"I love how you do that." His gaze was intense.

"Do what?" she asked.

"Take life as it comes to you. You don't wallow in the letdowns or tough times. You just keep it moving."

Siobhan shrugged, feeling both appreciative of and embarrassed by the praise. "Thank you."

Derick placed a kiss on her temple. "No, thank *you*. I sometimes struggle with that—letting life unfold as it will." He gave her a gentle squeeze. "You're a good influence on me."

She smiled at him. "Back at ya."

Afterward, they decided to walk down toward the water and watch the gentle waves lap onto the shore. Derick put his arm around her waist and pulled her in close.

She relaxed against him immediately. "I'm glad you're here."

"Me, too. You never would've found your way out of that enormous zoo without me."

She slapped his chest lightly and then left her hand there, pressed against his heart. "That's not what I meant, Captain Sarcasm."

He looked down at her, his expression soft and loving. "I know what you meant, baby."

And as Siobhan burrowed even closer to him, she was glad they were finally on the same page.

Chapter 11

EIGHT DAYS. THAT'S how long it had been since Derick had seen her. He'd had business to tend to in New York, and as much as it killed him to do so, he'd had to leave Siobhan. And now, as he stared out the back of the car and watched the dark, unfamiliar city flash by him, he couldn't believe he'd ever been able to go more than a month without seeing her.

He leaned back against the headrest and tried not to focus on what *had* been. Instead, he did his best to focus on what *was*.

Derick was on his way to see Siobhan. And he was only minutes away from the bar she had told him to go to. He'd missed her so much the past week he had half a mind to kidnap her back to his hotel room and keep her all to himself.

But he knew he had the next five days with her. He also knew how important it was for her to attend the celebration for one of her friends, who had recently landed a showing at a high-end handcrafted-furniture boutique. Art nouveau, Siobhan had called it. Derick pulled his phone out, thinking he should probably google what the hell that meant, but it was too late.

The driver pulled up in front of Cass Café, and Derick looked up at the nondescript tan stone building in front of him. It didn't seem to be anything like the large, artsy hangout he had pictured when Siobhan had told him about the place.

But when Derick pulled the door open, he knew he'd come to the right spot. The open space had an industrial feel, especially with the loft seating area above the main dining room. The restaurant doubled as an art gallery, which Siobhan had said made it more appealing to local artists.

Derick headed toward the bar on the left side of the restaurant and looked around for Siobhan. He smiled when he saw her, and her face lit up. She waved him over to where she stood with five other people.

"Derick," she said excitedly before pressing her hands against his chest and giving him a kiss. "You made it! Derick, this is everybody. Everybody, this is Derick."

Derick gave the group a nod and said hello. They all introduced themselves, and as he scanned the eclectic mix of people—wearing clothing that Derick could only classify as art hipster—he immediately felt out of place in his dark gray Henley and relaxed jeans.

"I'm going to grab a drink. What are you having?" he asked Siobhan. "I'll get you another."

"A sea breeze," Siobhan answered, and he headed to the bar.

He returned a few minutes later with a sea breeze for Siobhan and a beer for himself. "So who are we celebrating?" Derick asked. Siobhan hadn't even told him.

"Oh, sorry," Siobhan said. "Jacob." She pointed to the guy in ripped skinny jeans and a faded orange T-shirt.

Derick congratulated him and asked him a bit about his work. He might not understand art, but he understood furniture, and he was happy that he had something to contribute to the conversation.

A minute or so later, the shots he'd ordered arrived. "Tequila okay?" he asked everyone as the server handed them over.

"Siobhan, why didn't you tell me your boyfriend was sexy *and* generous?" Jacob asked.

Derick laughed.

"Hey," Siobhan said, wrapping an arm around Derick's waist and squeezing him tightly against her. "Get your own man. This one's mine."

Jacob brushed the short dark hair on top of his head with his fingers and raised an eyebrow. "You don't happen to have a gay brother you brought with you, do you?"

"I don't," Derick said.

Jacob shrugged. "It was worth a shot."

The group toasted Jacob and then threw back the shots.

"Did Siobhan tell you about the gallery opening?" Daphne asked. "Jacob's not the only one who should be celebrating."

"No." Derick took a sip of his beer and turned to Siobhan. "Tell me."

"I just found out a few days ago, and I wanted to tell you in person." Siobhan was nearly bouncing with excitement. "A few of my paintings were displayed in a gallery. The opening went well, and the owner wants to keep my work up for a few months."

"She's being modest," Wendell said. "The gallery's been around a while, and Siobhan sold two paintings."

Derick beamed. "Really? That's fantastic."

Siobhan smiled. "I was lucky to even exhibit there."

"Luck had nothing to do with it," Jacob said. "You worked hard for that shit."

"Getting into this gallery's a big deal," Daphne added. "And it didn't just happen on its own. Siobhan's been doing a ton to get her work on different online retail sites and promoting it on social media. And it's definitely paid off."

Siobhan's cheeks flushed a bit. "I thought we were here to celebrate Jacob's show?"

"Looks like they want to celebrate your work, too," Derick said. He put an arm around her, pulled her in close, and leaned down to give her a kiss. "And it sounds like you deserve it."

The group talked for a little longer before they started to disperse, some roaming the restaurant to look at the art and others welcoming more friends as they arrived.

Siobhan introduced Derick to a few more of her friends before they finally decided to get a table and share a few appetizers. When a local band started to play, Derick asked her if she wanted to dance.

He wanted his hands on her.

The first song had a slow tempo, and Siobhan rested her head against his chest as he pulled her close. The two moved to the rhythm without speaking until Siobhan finally looked up at him. "Can I tell you something?"

Derick nodded. "Of course."

"Jacob was right. You *are* sexy."

The corner of Derick's mouth rose slightly, and he placed a soft kiss to her forehead. "I'm glad you think so." Then he dropped his head down so that it touched hers. He could smell the sweet drink on her mouth. He wanted to lick the taste off her.

His hands slid farther down her hips to her ass, which was only covered by the thin fabric of her dress. Siobhan giggled and tensed when he gave her a quick squeeze before bringing his hands back up to a place more suited for public viewing.

As the music played, they moved against each other, causing Derick's dick to harden with every soft brush of her body on his.

Her hands roamed up and down his back as she pulled herself harder against him, and he could tell she was as turned-on as he was.

Derick leaned down to whisper in her ear. "I think it's time we left."

"I think you're right," she said, before bringing her lips to his.

Chapter 12

DERICK STRAIGHTENED HIS clothing as he exited the car and headed toward the studio where Siobhan was finishing up a class. He hadn't seen her paint since that day in Central Park, so he was happy he'd arrived early to pick her up.

But as he opened the door, he didn't see Siobhan instructing the students. Instead, he saw her lying on a couch.

She wasn't the teacher. She was a nude model.

Chapter 13

AT THE SOUND of her name, Siobhan's head snapped up from its position. *Shit.* She knew that voice. She clutched the sheet that was loosely draped around her waist.

"Put this on," Derick said, thrusting at her the robe he'd grabbed off a nearby chair.

"Derick, I'm working. You weren't supposed to be here for another twenty minutes."

"Put the robe on, Siobhan." Derick's eyes blazed into hers, and she wasn't sure what emotions she saw in them. Confusion? Anger? Frustration? Protectiveness? Probably all of them.

At the sound of their voices, Michael came out from the back of the studio and approached Derick. "Is there a problem here?"

Siobhan didn't think it was possible, but somehow the question seemed to make Derick even more livid than he already was. "Oh, there's definitely a problem. Who the hell are you?"

"I'm the owner of the studio. Michael," he said. He extended his hand, but Derick didn't take it. "And you are?"

"I'm the guy who wants to know why the hell my girlfriend's lying naked on your couch," he said, stepping into Michael's space.

Michael turned toward the painters. "I think we're done for the day. Sorry, everyone."

Siobhan grabbed the robe and shoved it on. She didn't give Derick a second glance as she headed toward the back room to get changed.

She swung open the door to the dressing room, but when she went to close it before Derick could enter, he put a hand on the door to stop her. He followed her inside and closed it behind him. "What the hell are you doing?" he asked.

"What am *I* doing? I think I should be asking you the same question. You can't show up and make a scene like this. I'm working." Siobhan ran a hand through her hair.

"You're working naked. That Michael guy's paying you for your body."

"You say that like I'm a prostitute, Derick."

"I say that like I'm your boyfriend." His jaw tensed.

"Derick, among the art community, nude modeling is a respectable way to earn money. I get that you're upset, but other people—"

"You're not other people. You're my girlfriend. And I can't believe you're going to stand here and try to convince me that it's okay for strangers to look at my girlfriend naked. You can't really believe that."

Siobhan inhaled slowly, the scent of Derick's freshly showered skin invading her nostrils as he took a step closer to her. He had a point. And truthfully, she'd known that he wouldn't be happy when he found out about her side job. What boyfriend *would* be?

"I get why you're upset. But this was something I started doing before you and I got back together."

"Well, I think it's time you stopped." His voice was firm, but his tone had softened. "This," he said, bringing a hand up to slip inside her open robe, "is mine." He let his fingertips rest on her hip a moment before allowing them to brush over the skin of her stomach. "I'm the only one who gets to touch it." His amber eyes nearly hypnotized her as he spoke. "And I'd prefer it if I were the only one who got to look at it, too."

For once, Siobhan was speechless. The feminist in her wanted to protest, but she couldn't bring herself to. Derick's words brought a rush of wetness between her legs.

Then he trailed a hand up her ribs and over her breast, his fingertips grazing lightly over her nipple. "I know I can't tell you what to do, Siobhan. You're a grown woman, and you make your own choices." He brought his mouth down to her neck, and she instinctively tilted her head to give him access. "So I'm asking you," he said before his lips made contact with her skin to plant a gentle kiss. "Please don't do this anymore."

She felt herself go nearly limp in his arms as his breath

grazed her flesh, and a low moan escaped her. "Okay," she said softly.

Derick pulled back from where he'd been sprinkling kisses along her collarbone to look at her. He almost looked surprised. "Okay what?"

"Okay, I won't do this anymore."

A satisfied grin spread across Derick's face as his hand moved down her stomach to cup between her legs. He slipped one finger inside her and began moving his thumb in small circles over her clit. "Why?" he asked, bringing her closer to release with every stroke of his fingers.

Siobhan let out a shaky breath. "Because I'm yours," she answered softly.

"God, say that again." Derick's cock was hard against her thigh as he backed her into the wall.

"I'm yours, Derick."

Chapter 14

AS TURNED-ON AS Derick was, there was no way he was letting either of them get off in a place where Siobhan had just been naked in front of strangers. "Let's get out of here," he whispered before slowly withdrawing from her.

Her head whipped around. "Are you kidding me?"

Derick felt his lips quirk up in a smirk. "No."

Siobhan stared at him for a few seconds, her eyes narrowing more and more as the time ticked by. "You're blue-balling me."

A loud, raucous laugh burst out of him. "I wasn't aware that term could be used as a verb. But yes, I am."

"Why?"

The pout she was directing at him was almost too adorable for him to resist. Almost. He leaned toward her again but was careful not to make any physical contact as his mouth approached her ear. "I was under the impression that I was going to get to watch you paint. You'll get what you want when I get what I want."

"You want to watch me paint? Right now?" Her voice was filled with irritated disbelief.

She sighed loudly as she reached for her clothes. "I'm not sure how I feel about my boyfriend insisting that I put clothes *on*. Maybe I'm losing my touch."

"No. You lost *my* touch. And there's only one way for you to get it back."

He loved the sharp rise and fall of Siobhan's chest caused by his words. He hadn't ever played the dominant lover with her before, but he really liked it. And judging from the way she was staring at him and running her tongue over her lips, Siobhan liked it, too.

"My studio is closest," she said, her voice husky and breathless.

"Perfect."

She finished dressing, grabbed her bag, and led him out of the back room, through the room she'd never enter again if he had any say in the matter, and out onto the street. "It's close enough to walk."

So they did. As they headed to the studio, he was careful not to touch her as they walked side by side. The charged silence was clearly driving Siobhan insane.

The truth was, Derick couldn't think of anything else besides sex.

The two-block walk to her space seemed eternal. When she finally unlocked the door and let him in, his cock was ready to burst through his zipper.

He quickly took in the room: the floor-to-ceiling window that let in copious amounts of natural light, the easel set up by it with a blank canvas resting on it. A few paintings were leaning against the remaining walls. Truth be told, it wasn't much larger than his walk-in closet in New York, but it was obviously all the space she needed.

"A popular guy in the art scene here bought out this whole floor and made it into mini-studios. The rent is incredibly reasonable," she explained as she set her stuff down.

Derick nodded as his eyes took one more sweep of the room. Then he looked back at her. "Strip."

Siobhan grinned as she began slowly pulling off her clothes. "Are you going to draw me like one of your French girls?"

He stared at her, sure that confusion was plain on his face.

She rolled her eyes. "Haven't you seen *Titanic*? Leo? Kate Winslet?"

"Oh. Well, then, if you paint for me, I'll paint you."

Siobhan dropped her clothes onto the ground and stared at Derick for a long moment before turning and prepping her paints. Then she sat down in front of her easel, picked up a brush, and got to work.

Derick allowed himself to watch her paint nude for a few minutes. He took in the faint flush of her skin, the way she swept her hair around to one side so it rested softly on her breast. It was the most erotic thing he'd ever seen. She looked so comfortable. Painting was what truly brought out the light that Derick loved most about her. He'd never thought he could be more attracted to her. But watching her like that—seeing the vulnerability in every stroke across the canvas—made parts of him heat up in ways he'd never felt before.

Eventually, he moved up behind her, allowing his clothed body to press against her naked one. He felt her breath hitch, but she continued to make sweeping strokes against the canvas. Gently reaching around her, he dipped a finger into her paint.

He placed a soft kiss on the back of her neck before he shifted to give himself just enough room to run his paint-covered index finger down the soft slope of her spine.

She arched her back and inhaled sharply as the paint made contact. She dropped her hand from the canvas.

Derick reached around again and dipped both his thumb and his index finger. "If you stop, I'll stop," he whispered. "And trust me, you don't want me to stop."

A shudder raced through her before she lifted her paintbrush and continued.

Derick dipped the fingers of his other hand into the paint and then pressed his fingerprints into the skin on her hips. "I'm going to put my hands all over you," he said in a low, firm voice. He continued to dip his fingers and draw lines and press finger marks all over her back and sides. "That way, whenever you take your clothes off from now on, you'll remember the marks I put on you to claim what's mine. It'll be like my hands are still on you."

He moved to the side of her to paint around her nipples and over the taut flesh between and under her breasts, before streaking his fingertips down to her navel. Her brushstrokes were erratic, but she kept painting, even when he reached over her and left his fingerprints on the insides of her thighs as he pushed them open.

Derick took a moment to observe his handiwork: Siobhan covered in a variety of colors that his hands had put there. Plucking the brush out of her hand, he set it down and reached for a rag that hung from the easel. He wiped his hands as thoroughly as he could, and then he grabbed her by the hips, and twisted her on the stool until she faced him.

"I don't need my hands for the rest." He stepped between her spread legs. "You're going to undo my pants and pull out my cock. And then I'm going to take you in a way that'll leave no question about who you belong to."

Siobhan put her hands on his pants but didn't open them. Instead, she looked up at him. "Do you belong to me, too?"

Derick couldn't resist cupping her beautiful face. "I've never belonged to anyone the way that I've belonged to you. And I never will."

Her eyes misted over at his words, but she regained her composure quickly before deftly undoing his jeans and pushing them down along with his boxers.

Derick wasted no time pushing inside her. Her arms wound tightly around his neck as his hands drifted down to her ass. He spread his legs so he could thrust into her with all the power and need he felt coursing through him.

Siobhan was his. And he was damn sure going to make sure she knew it.

Loud gasps and moans filled the air as he bucked into her wildly. His thrusts were so intense he didn't dare remove one of his hands from where it was steadying her on her ass so that he could play with her clit.

It didn't seem like she minded.

"God, Derick, yes." Her hands fisted in his hair, pulling to the point of pain.

But the discomfort spurred him on. He wanted her wild. Feral. He wanted to imprint this encounter into her brain so that whenever she got the urge to run, she would remember this moment and know the truth: there was no longer any separating them. They were one.

She groaned loudly as he pumped his cock deep inside her.

Derick was all sensation, feeling everything but registering nothing but pleasure and overwhelming love for the woman in his arms.

Siobhan released a choked scream as she came, her wetness coating his cock as he continued to thrust it inside her.

His ass flexed hard as he delved as deeply into her and as hard as he could, his release rocketing out of his body and into hers. Burying his face in her neck, he shallowly pumped into her a few more times, letting her walls milk him. He wanted to leave every drop inside her.

They remained in their embrace for a bit longer, until the heat they'd generated dissipated and left their sweat-soaked bodies trembling in the coolness of the room. Pulling back only enough to look at each other, Derick placed a lingering kiss on Siobhan's lips.

When they finally pulled apart, Siobhan smiled. "So do you like my studio?"

Derick grinned back. "Hands down the best place I've ever been."

Chapter 15

SIOBHAN QUICKLY APPLIED some lip gloss and grabbed a light jacket before heading out the door to meet Derick, who had just texted to say that he was outside.

When she got to the street, she saw him standing by the car. But it wasn't the usual black SUV. It was some sort of steel-gray sports car that was so low to the ground she thought she might fall trying to get in. It wouldn't be the first time he'd have to catch her.

As Derick gestured to the raised passenger-side door for her to get in, Siobhan's confusion only increased. She leaned down to look inside, and then she stood upright and turned toward Derick. "Where's the driver?"

Derick's smile stretched nearly ear to ear. "You're lookin' at him."

It took a moment for Siobhan to register what Derick had said, but when she did, she choked out a laugh. "Seriously?"

"Yeah. Why do you seem so surprised?"

"Because you don't drive."

"I drive," he replied simply. "You've just never seen me do it."

Siobhan gave him a skeptical look and then took his hand and allowed him to help her in. "Whose car is this?" she asked, figuring he must have rented it, since he hadn't mentioned having any friends in Detroit.

He slid in next to her and started the engine. "I don't know," he said as he pressed on the gas, propelling the car forward. "But they're going to be really upset when they find out it's missing."

Siobhan's eyes widened, and she gripped Derick's forearm. "Wait, what?"

Keeping his eyes on the road, Derick remained silent for a moment, causing Siobhan's anxiety to intensify. Finally, at a red light, he turned toward her, amusement on his face. "It's mine," he said, laughing. "You actually think I'd steal a car?"

Siobhan thought for a moment. "I mean...no, not really."

He raised an eyebrow at her.

"Well, I *mostly* believed you wouldn't." Siobhan ran her hand along the smooth leather of the seat. "You had this brought out from New York?"

Derick nodded.

She'd never been impressed by a car before, but this one had her feeling differently. "What kind of car is it?" she asked. She'd never seen one with the driver's seat in between two other bucket seats, which were set back a bit.

"A McLaren F1. It has a top speed of more than two hundred thirty miles per hour."

Concern swept across Siobhan's face. She could sense Derick's excitement, but that only made her nervous. She felt her hands tighten on her thighs. "You're not going to go that fast, are you?"

Derick shifted gears, and Siobhan's body pressed against the back of her seat as the car accelerated. "There's no way we can go *that* fast on a public road," he said.

Siobhan relaxed a bit.

"But I don't exactly intend to obey the speed limit, either." There was a recognizable twinkle in his eyes when he took them off the road to glance at her. His hands rested comfortably on the wheel.

"You like driving, huh?"

The question caused a childlike smile to spread across Derick's face. "Is it that obvious?" he asked as he headed onto the highway and slid over to the left lane.

"Just a little." Siobhan let her head fall back against the headrest as she turned toward him. "It's cute."

"I don't get to drive much living in the city, so every now and then, I take one of my cars out and just cruise. When I can get out on an open road, it makes me feel free. Like I can somehow focus on everything and nothing all at the same time." Derick put a hand on her thigh and squeezed, looking over at her. "That probably doesn't make a ton of sense, does it?"

Although Derick had looked back to the road, Siobhan continued to stare at him. "This may seem crazy, but I actually know exactly what you mean. It's how I feel when I paint."

Despite the car's speed, Siobhan began to relax. He seemed more than in control of the car. And it drove so smoothly she hardly noticed they were going…*a hundred and five miles an hour. Jesus Christ.* She was thankful they were beyond the city limits so there wasn't any traffic or cops in sight.

She'd never gone that fast before, but it didn't seem to bother Derick, who changed the radio station as if he were cruising down a suburban street at twenty-five miles an hour.

"Marnel told me about her party yesterday. You excited to go?" he asked her.

"Yeah, it'll be great to see the girls again. You're coming too, right?"

"Yup," Derick said. "Wouldn't miss it."

Somehow Derick's comfort seemed to radiate through her as he drove. Finally, her muscles relaxed, and she let her clenched fingers straighten. "So where are we going?" she asked, looking out into the clear night sky.

Derick took a hand off the stick shift and placed it over hers, threading their fingers together. "Nowhere special."

Siobhan focused on the feel of Derick's hand over hers as he rubbed her skin gently with his thumb. She recognized the familiar pull in her stomach at even such an innocent touch. And somehow she could sense that he felt it, too.

She ran her fingernails up Derick's arm and let out a slow breath as his hand moved to scratch the inside of her thigh over her jeans. Her hips rose slightly in a silent plea for him to move higher.

He complied. But as his hand rubbed over the seam of her jeans, it only teased her more. The sloped angle of the seat and the fact that it was set back from his would prevent him from giving her the stimulation she so desperately craved.

She could feel how soaked her underwear already was just from Derick's hand toying with her over the thick fabric of her jeans. He continued the delicious pressure on her clit, and it had her moaning softly as her ass tensed and she begged for more. "Jesus, Derick, I need you to touch me," she said, reaching over to grip his cock, which was firm against his pants.

Derick groaned, and Siobhan could tell how difficult it was for him to focus on the road while she was massaging his shaft, stroking him a few times before moving her palm over the tip and back down again. "Are you trying to make me come in my pants, Siobhan?" he asked playfully as his head hit the headrest.

"That depends," she said. "Are you going to make me come in mine?"

Derick hit the gas harder as the car in front of him moved to the right to let him by. "No," he answered. "I thought I'd have *you* do it."

Siobhan's stomach was nearly in her throat. Whether it was from Derick's driving or the sexual torture he was inflicting on her, she wasn't sure. She released a shaky breath as he withdrew his hand from between her legs and placed it back on the wheel.

"Unbutton your jeans," he said, nodding toward her but keeping his hands on the wheel.

Siobhan did as he instructed and dragged the zipper down, too.

"I want you to do to yourself what you wish I could do to you." Derick chanced a glance at her and then directed his gaze back to the highway. "And I want you to describe it to me because I can't look at you."

The sound that came out on Siobhan's exhale sounded almost like a laugh.

"What's funny?"

"I don't know if I can do this."

"Do what?" Derick asked. "Make yourself come? Or describe it?"

"Both. Or at the same time, maybe. I don't know." She shook her head.

"I'd like you to try." Derick's eyes remained fixed on the road. Then he patted her on the leg and smirked. "I have faith in you."

"Oh." Siobhan laughed. "Well, that's encouraging."

"You've done it before, right?"

"Masturbated in a car? Nope. Surprisingly, this is my first time," she deadpanned.

Derick gave her a chastising glance. "Stop being a smart-ass and touch yourself."

This time, Siobhan complied, sliding a hand under her shirt to run her fingers above her panties. She moaned as she moved the other hand up to her nipple, pulling gently.

"What are you thinking about?" Derick asked.

"I'm pretending it's your hand on my stomach, your mouth on my breast."

"Keep going. Tell me what you'd want me to do to you."

She thought for a few seconds, but she didn't feel as embarrassed vocalizing her desires as she thought she would. "I'd want you to go lower, Derick....Put your fingers inside me....Rub me," she said, slipping a hand below her white lace thong. "You'd feel how wet I am for you."

Siobhan kept her eyes open, watching Derick as he moved a hand to his cock and pulled slowly. She moaned softly at first, but the sounds grew louder and wilder as her fingers drew small circles over herself. She shifted her position a bit and thrust upward at her own touch.

Derick put both hands on the wheel to pass the car in front of him. "Did you touch yourself like this after you left New York?"

She didn't expect the question, so she answered truthfully. "Not at first."

"Why?"

"I didn't want to think about you when I left," she admitted. "This would've reminded me of you. The way you put your hands on me, inside me," she said, pushing a finger inside herself.

"But eventually you did?"

Siobhan exhaled heavily as her fingers slipped over herself. She was so wet she almost couldn't give herself the friction she needed. "Yeah."

"What changed?" Derick asked, gripping himself again.

She watched him tug hard on his cock under the material of his pants, and she wished she could see it. She loved the way it looked when he was ready like this, the tip nearly purple and beaded with moisture.

"I needed this," she answered, "and I didn't care if it made me think of you." The speed of her hands increased as she felt herself get closer. "I love when you move your fingers like that, when you stroke the inside of me," she said, doing it to herself but knowing she could never replicate the feel of Derick's fingers.

"God, Siobhan, you're going to make me come." He let out a short, choppy breath as his movements slowed. "Listening to you talk to me like that…I can't take much more."

Siobhan rode her own hands shamelessly now, needing the release she knew was imminent. Her eyes closed as her muscles began to tense, until finally, she clenched around her fingers, her body pulsing as her orgasm spread through her.

She came down from it slowly, and when she had recovered, she unbuckled her seat belt and slid up to the front of her seat.

"What are you doing?" Derick asked, as Siobhan undid his pants to let his cock spring free.

"Giving you road head," she said, as if the answer were obvious. It should have been. "I've always wanted to do this, and now seems like the perfect opportunity."

"Siobhan, we're going over a hundred miles an hour."

She smiled at him before licking her lips. "Then I'd better make this fast. Keep your eyes on the road," she said, before dropping her head to his lap and enveloping him in her mouth.

Derick gasped as his tip hit the back of her throat.

She moved over him wildly, her tongue slipping over his shaft. When his hips flexed, she knew he was close. It wasn't long before he was coming, shooting long bursts of semen into the back of her mouth.

Derick's body tensed with his release. But after he'd fully emptied himself into her, his muscles loosened, and his rigid body relaxed. She lifted her head and helped him fix his pants before she settled into her seat and buckled herself back in.

The two stared at the road ahead of them for a few minutes in quiet satisfaction.

Chapter 16

"ARE WE THERE YET?" Siobhan asked Derick again. She'd posed the same question every time she'd felt the driver stop the car.

"I could get used to this," Derick said.

"Used to what? Me acting like a four-year-old on a road trip? I was hoping it would be annoying and you'd eventually give in and tell me where we're going."

"Nope. That part's definitely annoying. I was talking about this," he said, tugging gently on the blindfold he'd put on her. Then he pressed his mouth to hers, parting it gently with his tongue. She hadn't anticipated it coming, and it made the feeling even more erotic.

"Do that again," Siobhan said when he broke contact.

"I can't. We're here."

By the time the car came to a stop and she heard a door open, Siobhan was bouncing with anticipation again. Derick got out first and took Siobhan's hand to help her out of the car. "Where is *here?*"

"You'll find out in a minute."

"Can I take the blindfold off?"

"Not yet," he said. She heard him unlock a door, and then he guided her inside. She recognized the lingering smell of fresh paint but still had no clue where they were, other than that they were in an elevator.

When it stopped and the doors slid open, Siobhan felt Derick untie the blindfold carefully and then remove it so she could see.

He came around from where he'd been standing behind her and exited the elevator, grasping her hand so she could walk with him. "What do you think?" he asked as he gestured around them.

Siobhan took in her surroundings—the high ceilings, the clean white walls, the floor-to-ceiling windows and exposed brick. The place was sparse in terms of furniture, but she knew exactly what this was. "Oh, my God! You rented an apartment here?"

"Don't be ridiculous. I bought it," he said, with that disarming smile she loved.

"You *bought* it? You're only commuting back and forth. You don't need a permanent residence here."

"I might. I don't know when, or even if, you'll decide to move back to New York." Derick shrugged. "Plus, I got a good deal on the place."

Siobhan quirked a lip up. "I didn't know you were such a bargain shopper."

Derick chuckled as Siobhan moved toward the kitchen. She ran her fingers along the cool light-gray granite. "I like it," she said, thinking how much it resembled his place in New York. "I think you need more than just a couch and a TV, though."

He followed her over to where she'd leaned against the counter. His hands found her hips as he stood in front of her and pressed against her, "I have a bed, too."

Slipping her arms around him, she raised her eyes to find his. "Are you trying to seduce me?"

"That depends. Is it working?"

Siobhan gave him an amused grin and a sharp slap on the ass. "What part of the city is this, anyway?" she asked, disengaging herself from him and heading over toward the windows.

"Midtown."

She moved across the hardwood floor of the main living space and looked down at the street below. She was surprised that they were only a few floors up and not at the top of a penthouse in a high-rise.

But upon closer examination, there was something that surprised Siobhan even more. She recognized the surrounding buildings. She knew exactly where Derick's apartment was located.

"Oh, my God," she said, her eyes wide as she brought a hand up to cover her mouth. "*You* bought the building so the mural wouldn't be destroyed?"

Chapter 17

DERICK STUDIED SIOBHAN'S expression before answering, but he couldn't discern anything from it. "I may have done that, yes."

That was when Siobhan showed what she was feeling. But there were many emotions flitting across her face so quickly that he couldn't get a handle on any of them. She turned back to the window and stared down at the bustling street below with her arms crossed over her chest.

After a couple of silent minutes, he moved up beside her. He shoved his hands into his pockets as he looked down at the street with her. "Siobhan, can you please say something?"

He chanced a glance at her. Her brow was furrowed, and her arms were wrapped around herself.

"I'm trying to figure it out." Her voice was so low he wouldn't have heard her if they hadn't been alone in the apartment.

"Figure what out?" He was afraid of her answer. Bone-shakingly, nail-bitingly afraid.

She turned to face him, dropping her arms as she shifted. "I didn't tell you about this building until after you got here. I'd been working with a group of friends to save it for months before that, before we got back together. Before you ever showed up at my door."

Siobhan was clearly fitting the pieces together and wasn't liking the picture she was uncovering. Derick didn't want to make matters worse by talking, so he waited for her to connect the remaining dots.

She drew her shoulders back. "How did you know, Derick? How did you know I was trying to save this building?"

Derick lowered his gaze to the floor for a moment before meeting her eyes. "I really don't think you're going to like my answer," he muttered.

"I'm pretty sure I won't, either. But I have to know."

Even though Derick had known they'd probably end up having this conversation when he showed her the building, he still wasn't sure of the best way to avoid being flayed alive by her afterward. "I made a few trips out to Detroit after you left."

"To spy on me?"

He took an involuntary step forward but stopped when she moved back. "No. Just to check in. You took off out of the blue and went to a city where you didn't know anyone. I was worried."

"But you didn't check in. I didn't even know you were here."

Derick rubbed a hand through his hair. "Okay, maybe *check in* was the wrong term."

"What would the right one be? *'Stalk'*?"

"Oh, come on, Siobhan. If you were really that concerned about disappearing, you should've made your Facebook profile private."

Siobhan's eyes narrowed. "I use my Facebook to promote my art. I can't do that if it's private." She sighed and looked back out the window. "So is that how you found me initially? By trolling my profile?"

Derick extended his hands out to his sides and then let them fall against his thighs with a slap. "You want to know all of it, fine, here it is. I made it about two weeks before I went to Brooklyn and knocked on your door to hash things out. I didn't want to give in, but I missed you like crazy, and I was miserable. I went to your place, but when I got there, you didn't answer. So I waited and waited and waited, until finally, a neighbor told me you'd moved out. Imagine how I felt to know that not only had you left me, but you'd also left the city. Hell, the state."

Derick started pacing. The memory of it still ate at him. "So I went to the Stone Room. The girls confirmed that you had left, but they wouldn't tell me where you went." He stopped and pointed at her. "Those are some damn good friends. CIA operatives are easier to break."

Siobhan seemed to struggle to suppress a smirk at that, but he didn't let his gaze linger long, needing to move again. "So

I checked your Facebook. And there you were—in Detroit. You liked an event and commented that you'd be attending, so I flew out here and showed up. It turned out to be a rally for this building."

He stopped in front of her, needing her to understand what he had done and why. "My plan was to approach you and get you to talk to me. But when I got there, you looked so...happy. You were upbeat and relaxed. You never looked that way in New York. And I didn't want to ruin it. So I watched. And the more I watched, the more I saw how much this building meant, not just to you but to everyone there. They were fighting for it because they loved the mural on it. And I figured, if it wasn't the right time to fight for you, at least I could fight for something that meant something to you. To you and all your friends. So I bought it."

Derick shook his head. "Maybe it's stupid, but I figured if I could save the building, then maybe I could save us, too."

Siobhan's eyes darted to the ceiling and around the room as they misted over. She took in a shaky breath and let it out slowly. "It's not stupid. Well, I mean, it's kind of stupid." She rubbed her hands over her face and turned her back on him. "God, I don't know. This is all so confusing."

Derick stepped around her and pulled her hands away from her face. "Siobhan, talk to me."

Siobhan let out a small laugh, but it was a pained sound. "I don't know what to say."

"Well, start by telling me how you feel about what I just told you."

"That's the thing, I don't *know* how I feel. I knew you had to have looked me up somehow. Obviously. You showed up at my apartment. You had to have done some digging. But I didn't expect you to say that you came here and watched me for weeks before you got in contact with me. And I'm mad about that but not as mad as I feel I should be, which only pisses me off more. I have a bunch of negative emotions about what you did, but there are positive ones, too. And I don't know what to do with them all, Derick. This is really overwhelming."

He bent down slightly so he could look her in the eyes. He saw the turmoil there, and it gutted him. "How can I make it better?"

"I think I just need some time to sort it all out. Maybe it would be best for me to go to Marnel's party alone. Get some space to sort through how I'm feeling, and then we can talk things out afterward."

"But we *will* talk things out?"

Siobhan brought a hand up and placed it on his cheek. "I've forgiven bigger things, Derick. Just give me a little time."

Chapter 18

SIOBHAN COULDN'T BELIEVE she was back in New York. She'd been in the city for about three hours, and she was already longing to leave as much as she had been months ago. It didn't help that every landmark she saw reminded her of Derick, whom she hadn't spoken to since their fight a few days earlier. She'd said she needed space, and she was determined to take it.

There was only one thing, well, one person, who could make her return better: Marnel. Siobhan had promised to come back for her birthday, so there she was, walking into the Stone Room, which had been rented out for the occasion—and not by Marnel. Siobhan needed to get the story behind that. That alone might make this trip worth it.

Siobhan gazed around the bar, thinking how different it looked from the hangouts she frequented in Detroit. The slate-gray couches matched some of the lighter tones of the stone walls, which gave the space an elegant but rustic feel. With its dark hardwood floors and smooth black bar, the

Stone Room screamed masculinity. But the delicate crystal lighting fixtures added a more feminine touch. When she'd worked here, she'd never really stopped to appreciate the beauty that surrounded her. Now it was all she saw.

As she craned her neck to look for familiar faces, she heard a screech that resembled a hyena being burned alive. Or at least that's what Siobhan imagined that would sound like.

"Oh, my God, I can't believe you actually came!" Suddenly, she was enveloped in Marnel's gangly embrace. And as Siobhan squeezed her back, she realized the trip was already worth it. She was still getting that story, though.

"Of course I came. I said I would."

Marnel pulled back, resting her hands on Siobhan's forearms. "I know what you said, but I also know how you Detroitians are."

Siobhan cocked her head. "And how *are* we Detroitians? And is that what we're really called?"

Marnel shrugged. "Hell if I know. But I picture they're all like Eminem in *Eight Mile*."

Siobhan nodded in feigned understanding. "So, hard workers with profound rap skills."

Marnel's smile widened. "Exactly."

Pulling her friend back into a hug, Siobhan said, "I missed you."

This time, it was Marnel's turn to tighten her arms. "We miss you, too, darlin'."

Tears prickled Siobhan's eyes, but she fought them. She

took a step back to get herself under control. "You a Southern belle tonight?"

Marnel smiled, but it seemed awkward and forced. "Nah, I'm just plain old Marnel. Who was Southern once upon a time but about as far from a belle as someone can get." There was no trace of the accent when she spoke this time.

Siobhan's eyes narrowed. This was all news to her. Marnel had never really opened up much about her past, and the only time she'd ever spoken with a twang was when she'd been playing a character. "Really?"

"Yup."

Siobhan opened her mouth to ask more but was interrupted when she saw Blaine and Cory running toward them. And while they squealed and hugged her, Siobhan kept her eyes on Marnel—someone she suddenly felt she didn't know as well as she'd thought, someone who was somehow both familiar and foreign.

"Where's Derick?"

Siobhan's eyes snapped to Cory. "What?"

"Derick. You know, the gorgeous billionaire who chased you to Detroit? Where is he?"

"Home, I guess." Siobhan shrugged, hoping her nonchalance would cause the subject to drop.

"Why the hell is he at home? He knew he was invited, right?" Blaine asked.

Siobhan's eyes drifted over the large crowd in the bar. "Let's talk about it later. I want to know all about the man who's throwing Marnel this party. And why he chose to have it where she works. Aren't you sick of this place?" She cast a sly glance toward Marnel, who blushed. Siobhan was getting weirded out. She'd never seen Marnel even remotely embarrassed during the months they'd worked together, and she'd seen Marnel do some epically dumb shit.

"Ooh, you want to know about Nate?" Cory taunted.

"Yes, I would *love* to know about Nate," Siobhan replied.

They trained their attention on Marnel, who was inspecting her freshly manicured nails with the focus of a brain surgeon. When the silence finally caused her to look up, she sighed loudly and smacked her hands against her thighs. "Stop staring at me. And I had it here so my friends wouldn't have to call off work to attend. A decision I'm suddenly regretting."

"Aw, that's sweet. And we're not staring. We're being attentive," Blaine explained.

Marnel shot them an exasperated look. "Attentive to what?"

"The story you're about to tell us. About Nate. Feel free to include all of the indecent things you're doing with him that would prompt him to rent out an entire bar for you." Blaine stepped forward, making their little circle tighter.

Marnel's eyes darted to each of them. She straightened, flicked a piece of her long blond hair over her shoulder, and said, "It's my party, and I'll ignore you if I want to." Then she stalked off into the crowd.

Siobhan turned to the girls. "So you guys don't know anything about him, either?"

"We know who he is." Cory pointed toward the bar. "He's the super-hot one with the light hair and dimples, in case you were wondering," she said with a teasing smirk.

Siobhan strained to see through the crowd to get a better look at him. "Oh, I see him now. He *is* super-hot."

"Well, now you know as much as we do. Something's obviously up, but she refuses to talk about it," Cory said.

Siobhan's eyes widened. "Marnel's being tight-lipped about something? That's…unfathomable."

Cory and Blaine nodded in agreement.

Conversation shifted to catching up with one another. Siobhan was feeling more relaxed than she'd been all week.

"Hey," Blaine said, drawing Siobhan's attention. "I thought you said Derick wasn't coming."

Siobhan felt her shoulders tense at the mention of Derick's name again. *So much for feeling relaxed.* "He's not."

"Then why is he walking this way?"

"What?" Siobhan yelped. She whirled around, but as she did so, her heel caught on the floor, causing her to stumble. And for the second time since she'd met him, Derick Miller saved Siobhan from falling flat on her face in the Stone Room.

Chapter 19

"WHY ARE YOU HERE?" Maybe some sort of gratitude for catching her was warranted, but she was too shocked to be tactful.

"I promised I wouldn't miss it," Derick replied simply, as he made sure she was steady and then let go of her arm.

She glanced toward the girls, who had silently retreated into the crowd. "I said I wanted to come alone."

"You did. And then I met you here," he replied with a small smile, his eyes averted in a way that reminded her of a young boy trying to get away with something.

Siobhan wanted to be indignant. To demand the time he had agreed to give her. But something about Derick in a well-tailored charcoal suit made the words die on her tongue. "You're really annoying, do you know that?"

"I may have been told that a few times in my life. But let's talk about you," he said, letting his gaze trail up and down her body. "*You* look really remarkable in red."

Siobhan tried not to glow at the compliment. She had to

admit she felt good in her form-fitting wrap dress. "That was very alliterative" was the only reply she could come up with.

Derick looked thoughtful. "I could also say you look ravishing. Refined."

Siobhan glared at him.

Derick snapped his fingers. "Radiant. That's how you look. Completely and utterly radiant."

Rolling her eyes, Siobhan had to fight hard to hold back her smile.

He rested his cheek against her temple, which put his mouth by her ear. "You're not still mad at me, are you?"

"No," Siobhan said, though even to her own ears it didn't sound all that convincing.

"Don't be mad at me anymore. It sucks."

Siobhan snorted. "How eloquent."

He drew back so he could look at her. "I mean it. I know I do some dumb stuff, but I can't take the silent treatment anymore. I'd rather have you yell at me than not talk to me at all."

Siobhan slid her arms around him. "I don't want to yell at you."

He drew her in tighter against him. "Good. Because I don't particularly enjoy that, either."

It took her a minute to realize they were dancing. The firm press of his body against hers as they swayed to the delicate notes of the music was intoxicating.

But then his words ruined it. "So, just to be clear, you're not mad, or you are?"

Siobhan couldn't help it—she burst out laughing. "Loving you is infuriating sometimes."

The serious look on his face sobered her. For all of his swagger and confidence, the beautifully irritating man in front of her truly did need to know the answer to his question. In that moment, Siobhan realized that as much as she was enchanted by Derick, she held the same power over him. It was equal parts empowering and terrifying.

She tightened her embrace around him. "No, Derick. I'm not mad."

Chapter 20

"WHAT TIME IS IT?" Siobhan asked.

Blaine pulled her phone out of her bag. "Quarter after eleven."

"Really?" Siobhan's eyes widened. She couldn't believe she'd already been at the party for almost three hours. "I feel like I just got here."

Cory took another sip of her wine. "Nope. We've been drinking for hours. I promise."

Marnel steadied herself against the bar stool. "Then why am I not drunker?"

Blaine raised an eyebrow. "I don't think *drunker* is a word," she said. "And you're drunk enough. You look like you're a cheeseburger away from a remake of that David Hasselhoff video."

"Stop." Marnel gave Blaine a shove, but it only made Marnel even more off balance than she already was. "I'm not that bad." She flipped her hair and straightened her dress. "Enough about me. Siobhan, tell us how things are going in Detroit."

Siobhan finished the last bit of her drink and set the glass on the bar. "They're good."

"That's all you've got for us?" Cory said. "'They're good'?"

Siobhan smiled and lifted her shoulders in a shrug. "There isn't really much to say that you guys don't already know. My art is still selling, which is awesome, obviously." She thought for a moment. "I still have great friends and a shitty apartment. Oh," she said, remembering something she hadn't told them yet. "Derick bought a place out there."

"Seriously?" Blaine asked. "Is he moving there?"

"Nah, just commuting back and forth. I guess he thought it was stupid to keep staying in a hotel when he has no idea how long he'll have to keep flying out there. He figured he'd invest in something more permanent." For the first time since she and Derick had gotten back together, Siobhan felt a twinge of guilt about what Derick was sacrificing to keep their relationship going. Sure, he had the money and time to make the frequent trips. But flying back and forth every few days had to be exhausting. And yet he hadn't once complained or asked her again about her thoughts on moving back to New York.

Siobhan and the girls had another drink and chatted about the Stone Room and the new band Cory had hitched up with on vocals. They even tried to press Marnel for more information on Nate. But she slurred a "Wouldn't you like to know" before excusing herself with a smirk and heading over to where Nate was talking with some other guys.

"I'm going to grab a drink for Derick," Siobhan said,

pointing to where he was standing across the room with two people. "You guys want anything?"

They both declined.

When Siobhan walked up next to him, Derick put an arm around her and gave her a light kiss on her temple. "Thanks," he said, putting his nearly empty glass on the table before taking the beer Siobhan had brought over.

He introduced her to the two people he'd been speaking with, and the four of them talked for a few minutes before the other couple headed to the bar for refills.

"Thank God," Derick said once they were out of earshot. "Those people were crazy. The woman told me how she collects porcelain doll heads. She puts them on her windowsills facing outside to ward off evil spirits."

Siobhan laughed. "Only you would get stuck talking to someone like that. Who were they?"

Derick slid a hand casually into his pocket. "I have no idea. They just came over to me and started up a conversation."

"That's because you have one of those faces."

Derick lifted an eyebrow, prompting Siobhan to continue.

"You look approachable. You smile a lot. And you make eye contact with strangers," she explained. "That's always a big mistake in New York."

Derick chuckled.

"See? That's the face right there. Your eyes get all crinkly, and you look happy."

Derick's face sobered a bit, and he reached a hand up to

the back of Siobhan's neck as he stared into her eyes. "I *am* happy," he said.

Siobhan gazed at him, his deep amber eyes sparkling in the dim overhead lighting. "So am I."

A few silent moments passed between them before Derick's mouth was on hers, sliding it open with his tongue and pressing her back against the stone wall behind her. It was a sweet, slow kiss, but when he pulled away, it left her breathless and wanting more. "Why'd you stop?" she whispered.

Derick threw his head back toward the people behind him. "The party isn't over. And if I don't stop, I'm gonna want to touch more than the back of your neck. I figured you might appreciate some privacy for that."

Siobhan licked her lips before pulling on her bottom one with her teeth. "Privacy's overrated."

Chapter 21

DERICK'S COCK HARDENED instantly at the implication of Siobhan's words. There was no way she'd be okay with him taking her against the wall in front of an entire party of people. But the image excited him just the same. The thought of her skin warm against his as he pushed inside her had his whole body aching for her.

He pulled back to look at her, taking in her gentle eyes, her soft lips. "Dance with me," he said, his voice deep with desire.

He didn't wait for her to answer, and instead, he took her hand and led her out to the middle of the Stone Room, where the tables had been cleared for a dance floor.

Their dance started off innocently enough, with Derick's hands sliding over her hips as she moved seductively in front of him to the music. His pulse raced as he watched the smooth sway of her hips and the curves of her breasts as she danced. It was an image built for fantasies. "God, you're sexy," he said.

He let his fingers trace over the soft skin of her arm and

down to her hand, pulling it up to kiss it before spinning her around so her ass was against him. He stifled a groan at the contact, though he wasn't sure why. The hot flush of her skin told him Siobhan was enjoying this just as much as he was.

Despite the other people moving all around them, he felt like they were alone. The music drowned out everything but the two of them.

Her ass slid lightly over his cock as she moved against him, and his entire body seemed to catch fire at her touch. His hands roamed every inch of her they could reach, and he brought one of them up to sweep her hair off her exposed shoulder so he could kiss her neck.

Her skin was warm and salty from a thin sheen of sweat. He wanted more. God, he wanted all of her. "You keep rubbing that tight little ass of yours against me, and I'm gonna smack it."

She released a sound that was somewhere between a moan and a laugh. "Is that a promise?" she asked, never breaking contact with him.

She turned her head back toward him enough that he could kiss her. But this time, the kiss wasn't slow or gentle. Her fingers tangled in his hair as he devoured her. *Jesus.* She tasted sweet, like fruit and candy and summer.

His hands skated down her abdomen to her legs and back up again. And she moaned when his fingers touched the insides of her thighs.

"You like that?" he asked.

"Why do you always ask questions you know the answers to?" Her voice was playful, and it only turned him on more.

"Because I like to hear the answers," he replied. "I like to know what I do to you." His mouth moved to her bare shoulder and then to her bicep as he lifted her arms above her head. "So tell me," he urged. "What do I do to you?"

Siobhan turned to face him, her body still moving to the rhythm as she slid her arms around his neck and pressed her chest against him. She tilted her head back so she could look up at him. "You want to know what you do to me, do you?" she teased.

Derick nodded slowly before dropping his forehead to hers.

"You drive me completely nuts," she answered.

Derick smiled. That wasn't news to him.

Her expression morphed slowly into a more serious one. "You make me feel things I didn't know I was capable of feeling."

Derick pressed an innocent kiss on her lips.

"You dominate my mind. And my body."

That thought had Derick's erection stiffen harder against her. "I wanna do that right now," he said.

Siobhan bit her lip and slid her hands down Derick's arms until her fingers intertwined with his. "Follow me," she said, turning toward the hallway that led to the kitchen.

Siobhan opened a door off to the side, and Derick entered behind her. He didn't even stop to take in much of the office they were in before he was on her, pressing her against a wall, his mouth roaming all over her skin with heated urgency.

She was always so quick to respond. God, he loved that about her. How just the slightest touch would have her moaning and begging for more. "I need this," she said, gripping the hard bulge in Derick's pants.

Just that small bit of contact had him ready to explode.

Siobhan moved her other hand down, undoing his pants and sliding her palm over his boxers. She gripped him through the fabric, massaging his shaft and moving around his tip, which was already slick with his need for her.

The groans that came out of him were wild and unrestrained. For a few minutes, they were like teenagers, their hands caressing, groping each other frantically, like they couldn't get enough. Then Derick's hands were on her ass, hiking up her tight dress so he could rub the smoothness of her skin. With one quick movement, he lifted her off the ground, opening his eyes just long enough to carry her over to the large mahogany desk in the middle of the room.

Shoving some papers out of the way before her body made contact with the wood, he set her down on the desk.

When her hands went back to his cock, Derick nearly lost it. The urge to come was almost unbearable.

Her eyes were fixed on him as he pulled the fabric down to free himself, his cock heavy in his hand. His hands moved to her thighs, pulling her toward him suddenly so that the tip of his dick touched the lace of her thong.

God, he wanted her. He could feel how wet she was even through the fabric. The sounds that came from her—shallow pants and gentle whimpers—had him grinding against her until he couldn't take it anymore.

Derick pulled her off the desk and spun her around to face it, his shaft pressing into the crease of her ass.

"Jesus, Derick, I love that." She was already bent over the desk, her hands gripping the edge in front of her as she ground back into him. "Fuck me. Please." She huffed. "I can't take much more of this."

That was all Derick needed to hear before he shoved her panties to the side and thrust into her hard, feeling the warm, soft flesh inside her stroking him. With every drive, he jerked her hips toward him, pushing deeper each time, until he was practically lost inside her.

His eyes raked over her body, from the taut muscles of her back down to the curves of her hips. He withdrew almost completely and gave her ass a sharp crack with his palm.

Obviously not expecting it, she seemed to startle at the contact, but her satisfied moan told him she enjoyed it.

His movements grew faster, wilder, with each and every thrust inside her. He could feel his orgasm sliding down his spine, and he knew he couldn't hold off much longer. Especially when he could feel Siobhan tightening around his cock as she got closer, too.

"Touch me," she said. Her voice was small, a soft plea for him to give her what she needed. And Derick intended to. He slid a hand around her hip until his fingers reached their destination. He moved them in soft circles over her clit, causing her body to nearly quake from the contact.

"Yes. God, yes." She let out the words between heavy breaths as she rubbed herself against his hand.

He gave a few more hard thrusts before Siobhan screamed out, her body shaking with her release. At last he could allow himself to let go, to pound into her with unrestrained force until he came. His cock pulsed inside her as long bursts of semen shot from him. It was harder than he'd come in a while, and his legs nearly gave out beneath him with his release.

Before he withdrew from her, he placed a light kiss on her neck. "We should get back out there," he said. "The girls will probably wonder what we're doing."

Siobhan's lip quirked up into a hint of a smirk. "Oh, I think they have a pretty good idea," she said.

And then Derick was smiling, too.

Chapter 22

SIOBHAN FELT DERICK tighten his grip around her and press his nose into her hair. She wiggled against him, and he chuckled. "I guess that means you're awake."

She turned toward him and smoothed a hand up and down his chest. "Yup." She gave him a quick peck on the lips. "Last night was fun."

Derick smiled. "Which part?"

"Every part."

He pulled her flush against him. "That's what I like to hear." He began placing kisses along her jaw.

Siobhan sighed in contentment. "I forgot how much fun New York can be."

Derick pulled back and looked at her. "We've had some good times here."

She smiled. "We have." She left the words *but we've had more bad ones* unspoken, though she wondered if Derick's mind had gone there, too.

"We should stay."

"What?" Her body tightened with tension.

He moved a hand to her ribs and dug in slightly, making her writhe and laugh. "Not like that. I mean we should stay a few more days. Do some of the things we never got to do before."

She thought for a minute. *Before* was a loaded word that encompassed so many things. Before she'd left him. Before she'd run from New York. Before she'd lost herself and escaped to Detroit to reclaim who she was. Before he'd found her. Before she'd realized that loving—and being loved by—Derick was something she didn't want to be without ever again. "Okay."

Derick looked surprised. "Really?"

"Yeah, why not? I'm in no hurry to get back. So if you have the time, I have the time."

"Great." He smiled against her lips as he pressed them together. His hands started to roam over her body, and she couldn't help the moan that escaped her.

She began gyrating against him, reveling in the feel of his hard cock against her belly. She wrapped one leg around him in an attempt to get closer. Just as she got him right where she needed him most, his phone rang.

"You getting that?" she breathed into his ear.

"Hell, no," he replied before sucking on the soft skin of her neck.

The ringing stopped, only to start up again.

Siobhan rolled onto her back. "You'd better get it."

Derick sighed and reached for his phone on the bedside table. He looked at the screen and then sat up quickly. He glanced over at her. "I need to take this."

"Okay," Siobhan said, drawing the word out as she watched him get out of bed and walk toward the bedroom door. Her brow furrowed. She couldn't remember a time when Derick had avoided taking a call in front of her before.

He said a clipped "Hello" into the phone before leaving the room, closing the door behind him.

Chapter 23

"I'M SORRY TO bother you, Mr. Miller. But we've got a small problem."

Derick rolled his eyes and took a deep breath. "It's no problem, Liza. What's the issue?"

"The men you hired never showed up. The project isn't even close to being finished, and we're running out of time."

Derick pinched the bridge of his nose. He really didn't need this shit right now. Especially not with Siobhan in the next room. "Do you know anyone else who can do the job? Money isn't an issue. I want this finished. Yesterday."

"I could make some calls," Liza said.

"Good. Tell them there's a bonus in it for them if they make it their top priority."

"You got it."

"Send me an e-mail with the information for the new firm."

"Will do. Enjoy your day, Mr. Miller."

"You too, Liza." Derick disconnected the call and tossed the phone onto the couch.

Closing his eyes, he let out another sigh and willed the irritation out of his body. Once he was calm, he returned to the bedroom. And to a confused-looking Siobhan. *Shit.*

"Everything okay?" she asked, a wariness in her voice he wished he could relieve with the truth, but that was definitely not an option.

Plastering a smile onto his face, Derick slipped back into bed. "Sure. Just some drama with an app I'm helping develop. The creators are a bunch of drama queens."

Siobhan nodded, but it was slow and mechanical.

The last thing he wanted was to cause Siobhan to doubt him. He'd have to get her mind off it by other means.

He pulled her to him, and she obliged, sprawling half on top of him. "Now, where were we?"

Her lips quirked. "I'm not sure I remember."

Derick's eyes widened in mock surprise. "Was I that forgettable?"

She smiled as she stroked a hand down his cheek. "Nothing about you is forgettable."

Knowing his words would only ruin the moment, Derick tangled his hands in her hair and pulled her lips to his. There wasn't any urgency to the kiss. Their tongues danced together in a slow rhythm, soft moans punctuating the otherwise silent moment.

Derick rolled so Siobhan was under him before grabbing both of her hands and pinning them above her head. "Keep those there. I'm going to explore every inch of your body with my mouth, and I don't want to be distracted."

Siobhan groaned her acquiescence, her body bowing off the mattress as he trailed his fingertips along her skin.

He kissed and sucked on her neck before moving lower to nip at her collarbone. His large hands massaged her breasts before his mouth descended lower to lick her nipples. He flicked at them with his tongue, making her arch her spine and push her breasts toward him. He sucked the hard peaks into his mouth, causing her to gasp and writhe beneath him.

"Oh, my God, Derick. I need…" she panted.

He lifted his head slightly. "What do you need, Siobhan? Tell me."

"More."

"More of this?" he asked as he drew her nipple back into his mouth and his hand fondled the other.

Siobhan whimpered. "Of everything."

Derick smiled against her skin. "Don't worry, baby. I know what you need." His hand continued to pinch her nipple while he licked a path down to her belly button. He placed kisses on the taut flesh of her stomach, but he didn't linger long. This wasn't where she needed him.

When he finally reached her clit, he wasted no time in darting his tongue out to taste her there.

Once he made contact with the most erotic part of her, he felt her body tighten, saw her hands clamp down on the pillow above her head, and heard the soft "Oh, yes" that whispered past her lips.

He began to lick between her folds, sensing the orgasm building in the way her body responded to his attention. He wanted her climax on his tongue. Wanted to feel her lose control.

"I'm so close."

Derick hummed, a sensation Siobhan clearly liked, if her loud moan was any indication. He smoothed his hand up her thigh and brought it to her apex.

He dragged his thumb through her crease a few times before pushing it inside her. She let out a hoarse yell as he pumped his finger in and out of her while his mouth sucked harder on her clit.

Siobhan wriggled against his mouth, her breaths coming out in harsh gasps. She stilled briefly, and then shudders racked her body.

He continued to lick her, causing her to keep convulsing beneath him. When she relaxed into the mattress, he placed one last kiss on her before moving up her body.

She moved her hands and pushed them into his hair as he guided his cock into her. He was so turned-on it wasn't going to take him long to come.

He pumped into her, his hands digging into her hips to pull her into his thrusts.

"Yes. Come inside me, Derick."

Those words were all he needed. He thrust deep one last time as his dick pulsed his release into her.

He felt her come again, her walls flexing around his cock, helping to milk him dry. He thrust lightly a few more times, his lips taking hers in a punishing kiss filled with all the love he felt for her.

When their kisses had grown lazy and their breathing had returned to normal, Siobhan met his eyes and smiled. "There's one thing I'll say about New York. We have some epic sex here."

Derick joined in her laughter before interlacing his fingers with hers. "I'm pretty sure we have epic sex everywhere."

Siobhan leaned up to kiss him, the smile on her lips letting him know she agreed.

Chapter 24

REACHING OUT TO grasp Derick's outstretched hands, Siobhan cautiously pulled herself up into a standing position. She brushed the ice off her butt with one of her hands, while she kept a tight grip on Derick with the other. It was a routine she'd perfected over the last half hour or so while Derick tried to teach her to ice-skate. But that last attempt would be the last time she'd try to skate on her own without holding on to Derick.

She looked around at all the people on the rink, some of them children. "I feel like ice-skating is probably one of those things that you can't learn after a certain age. Like learning a foreign language or something."

Looking amused, Derick cocked his head to the side and smiled as he skated backward to guide Siobhan on the ice. "That's not true. Anyone can learn to skate. It's like riding a bike."

Siobhan steadied herself as she found her balance for the moment. "Don't even think about suddenly letting go. My dad did that when I first learned to ride a bike, and when I realized he wasn't holding on, I tipped over and cracked my head on the concrete of the church parking lot where we were practicing."

"Seriously?" Derick asked, and he glanced behind himself to make sure he wasn't going to run into anyone.

Siobhan nodded. "That's how I got this." She began to pull her hand from Derick's to touch the small indentation on her forehead right below her hairline, but she thought better of it. "I'll have to show you later," she said, laughing.

Derick squeezed her hands tighter and gave her a comforting smile. "I promise I won't let go."

His words soothed her. Not just because he wouldn't leave her to fend for herself on this slippery death trap but because she liked the idea of Derick holding on to her forever.

"I wouldn't want to traumatize all the children who would be forced to skate past your blood," Derick said, causing Siobhan to laugh out loud. They skated a little farther, and he asked, "So are you ready to kill me yet for making you come here?"

Siobhan's eyes narrowed. "I plan to take my revenge on you later tonight," she replied. But the truth was, despite falling on her ass in front of countless strangers, she was having a great time and was glad Derick had remembered that he'd wanted to take her skating at Rockefeller Center. She'd left New York without doing so many of the things the city had to offer.

Eventually, Siobhan let Derick release one of his hands so he could skate beside her. The two moved slowly, though still a little fast for Siobhan, whose legs wobbled beneath her. "What's next?" she asked, curious about Derick's plans, since he had wanted the day to be a surprise. Yesterday had been Siobhan's choice: the Guggenheim, Little Italy, and the Russian Tea Room.

"You're ready to call it quits already?" he asked, nodding toward her skates.

"It's probably best if I stop before I break anything."

"Fair enough," Derick said. "You did pretty well. Thanks for trying it."

Siobhan let go of his hand as they approached the side of the rink. She was thankful as soon as her skates touched ground that didn't feel slick. "It was fun. I actually did better than I thought I would." They sat down to take their skates off and put their shoes back on. "I'm just happy you didn't rent out the whole rink for some private lesson or something. The last thing I needed was everyone with a window seat in a restaurant watching me plop down like a toddler taking her first steps."

Derick laughed. "You know, I did actually consider renting it out. But it's Rockefeller Center. You gotta have other people there to get the full experience."

Siobhan smiled in agreement. Would she really come back a few weeks from now to visit again? If she didn't see the tree lighting this year, then would it be next year? Would she still be with Derick in this semi–long distance relationship a year from now?

She certainly couldn't picture her life without him. But was it realistic to think that they could continue this way indefinitely, with Derick flying to Detroit every chance he got and Siobhan coming to visit in New York on occasion? She shook her head slightly, deciding she'd rather not think about that right now.

"You hungry?" Derick asked, taking her hand and leading her out onto the street.

"I could eat something." Although they'd gone to breakfast earlier in the day, it was almost two o'clock, and they hadn't had anything since.

The subway ride took only a few minutes, and they walked another block to the place Derick had suggested. It was a café that served authentic Mexican food, including special desserts: homemade fried ice cream, churros, and chocolate tacos filled with caramel sauce, vanilla ice cream, and cinnamon.

They ate some lunch, and then Derick ordered one of the dessert samplers and some hot chocolate and brought it over to the bar that looked out onto the street. In between conversation, they ate slowly, enjoying the variety of flavors. Siobhan stared out the window, catching a vague reflection of herself in the glass.

She'd forgotten how much she loved to watch people, especially when she'd first moved to New York and hadn't been used to the rushed pace of the city and its inhabitants. She remembered how she used to wonder what each person's story was, why they were always in such a hurry, not stopping to take in the city surrounding them.

She nodded toward a middle-aged woman pulling back her graying hair. "What do you think her story is?" she asked Derick.

"Her story?"

"Yeah. Like where is she going? What does she do? That kind of thing."

Derick's eyes lit up. "Ooh, I like the sounds of this game," he said, although the woman was already out of sight. "I'm thinking she's on her way to get more cat food. She only has enough to feed six of them, and she doesn't want the other three to go hungry."

Siobhan elbowed him playfully. "That's mean."

"No way. The mean thing would be to let them starve," he replied, making Siobhan laugh out loud. "What do *you* think she's doing?"

Siobhan remembered the woman's hurried pace and the weariness in her eyes. "I think she's late for her shift at the hospital. She's a nurse. Long hours. She sees things she can't unsee. It's added years to her life." Siobhan's gaze remained straight ahead, but she could feel Derick's eyes on her.

"Well, that's cheerful," he said.

Siobhan huffed out a laugh through her nose as she turned to him. "Okay, your turn to pick someone."

Derick studied the people passing by the restaurant. "That

guy." He pointed to a gaunt-looking hipster in gray skinny jeans and a floral shirt that looked like it had been sewn out of a vintage curtain.

Siobhan thought for a moment. "I'm thinking he's running to a store to buy his girlfriend a last-minute anniversary gift because he didn't realize six months was something to celebrate." She looked to Derick. "What do you think?"

"No way he has a girlfriend," Derick said drily. "I think he's going out to buy a mirror so he can finally see what he looks like when he gets dressed in the morning."

Siobhan laughed. "I haven't done this since I first moved to New York."

"I haven't done this *ever*," Derick said.

"Well, I never actually played it out loud like that. I used to think about what New Yorkers' lives were like. I guess because I always wanted to be one so badly."

But at some point, the reality of living in the city that never sleeps had set in, and Siobhan had begun to understand that fast-paced way of life all too well. Eventually, though she wasn't exactly sure when, she'd stopped wondering what each person's story was.

Maybe it was because she'd gotten one of her own.

She was the girl who'd come to New York like so many others, leaving behind who they once were to find the person they hoped to become. An actor, a musician, a model, a writer, a dancer…a painter.

It hadn't taken her long to realize that all those who came

to New York brought with them the same thing: an unwavering optimism that they could beat the odds, that they could make a name for themselves in a place where so many people couldn't.

Why else would anyone move to a city where a shared studio apartment cost more than a mortgage payment on a three-bedroom suburban house?

Siobhan finished the last bite she could eat of the dessert, and Derick polished off the rest. He threw their trash away and held the door while Siobhan exited the café.

They decided to walk the three blocks toward Central Park. The zoo would be their last stop before heading back to Derick's.

Their pace was quick, purposeful. It made Siobhan feel like a real New Yorker—on a mission to get somewhere. Or maybe to get *away* from somewhere. The sounds were familiar ones: heels clicking on concrete, conversations melding together until they became one steady din of voices, the occasional fist pounding on the hood of a cab as a pedestrian tried to cross the street.

Sharp orange light pierced through the thin spaces between buildings, silhouetting them against the fall sky. She knew this moment well, the last few hours of light right before the sun goes down and the city comes to life, waking itself up with artificial neon lights and the almost imperceptible hum of jazz or blues from some bar only locals frequent.

She'd been gone a few months, had moved to a city she'd

grown to love and, more important, a city that loved her in return. But after a few days back in New York, she could already feel the thrum of the city pulsing inside her like a heartbeat she hadn't noticed had stopped.

The last time she'd been in the park had been for one of her painting classes. And come to think of it, she didn't think she'd ever actually gotten a chance to enjoy it when she wasn't working.

Their pace slowed when they entered the park, and everything looked different from how she remembered it. "It's beautiful here in the fall," Siobhan said. She wished she had her art supplies with her so she could properly capture the park's beauty.

Derrick's smile shone in his eyes when he spoke. "It's perfect."

Siobhan couldn't take her eyes off the scenery, as she tried to catch everything she'd somehow managed to miss when she'd lived here. "It really is," she said.

Chapter 25

DERICK WATCHED SIOBHAN put her toiletries into her suitcase and zip it up. He walked over to lift it from the bed and placed it by the door with the rest of their luggage.

"Guess that's it," Siobhan said.

"Looks that way."

Siobhan closed the small gap between them and slid her arms around his waist. "This was a good trip," she said, her cheek pressed against his chest.

Derick rubbed his hands up and down her back. "It was. Though I always have a good time when you're around."

Siobhan swatted his ass. "Suck-up."

Placing a chaste kiss to the top of her head, Derick replied, "You know it."

They broke apart slowly, and Derick pushed his hands into his pockets to resist pulling her back to him. "Where are you meeting the girls?"

"Some restaurant downtown. I told them we needed to

meet at eleven thirty. That should give me plenty of time to catch our flight, right?"

"Yup. The jet's scheduled for takeoff at four, so it shouldn't be an issue. I'm sure the captain won't mind waiting a few minutes if one of his two passengers is missing." Derick shot her a wink before walking over to the chair and taking his jacket off it. "My meeting should be all tied up by one, so I'll be there waiting for you."

"Hmm, that's how I like you best: waiting for me."

Derick walked over and ran his hand along her jaw. "I'll always wait for you."

Siobhan smiled, and Derick couldn't resist pressing a kiss to her lips.

He walked over to grab his keys and wallet from the table. When he turned back toward her, she was rubbing her hand over the back of the couch. "You okay?" he asked.

"Do you miss it?"

Derick's eyes narrowed in confusion. "Miss what?"

"Living here. Full-time, I mean. The commute has to be getting old."

Derick thought for a moment how best to answer her, and after releasing a small sigh, he decided the truth was it. "I don't love all the flying back and forth. But I do love you. So…you're worth it. Whatever I have to do to keep you is absolutely worth it."

She looked at him. "Let's make it six months."

He raised his eyebrows and waited for her to clarify.

"Once we've made it six months without breaking up, then we can talk about coming back to live in New York."

Surprise was probably evident on his face as he stood there and stared at her. There were a million questions floating around his brain. Was she sure? Didn't she love Detroit? He wasn't pressuring her, was he? Could she be happy here? Did she not think they'd make it six months?

But the only thing that actually came out was a simple "Okay."

Chapter 26

"UGH, THIS PLACE is so crowded," Cory said.

Siobhan went up on her tiptoes and scanned the foyer of the restaurant they'd chosen to meet at for a farewell brunch. "We might want to try somewhere else. I have to meet Derick at the airport at three."

"There's another place two blocks up that I've been to a few times. It's a hole in the wall, but their food's pretty good," Marnel said.

Blaine shrugged. "Works for me."

The women walked back out into the chilly New York air, pulling their coats tighter around them.

"You excited to get home?" Cory asked.

"Yeah, I guess. It's definitely been nice visiting, though. I left New York in such a bad place, I forgot how great it can be here." Siobhan was nearly overwhelmed by the feeling of having come full circle. And even though she didn't want to admit it out loud, the city felt more like home than she'd initially allowed herself to admit. Maybe moving back here with Derick one day wouldn't be such a bad thing.

"Oh, they're finally filling this empty store space. There hasn't been anything here in a while," Blaine remarked.

Siobhan threw a cursory glance at the renovated storefront. And then she looked again. Stopping abruptly, she barely registered Marnel walking into her.

"Jesus. Warn a girl, would ya?" Marnel joked.

Siobhan took a step closer to the large window. *It can't be.*

She felt a hand on her arm. "Siobhan? What's wrong?"

Never averting her eyes from the window, Siobhan wasn't even sure who had spoken. The words that came out of her mouth weren't directed at anyone, either. "The paintings."

Cory's reflection stood next to hers in the window. "You don't like them? I think they're amazing."

Siobhan finally let her eyes leave the paintings so she could turn her head toward Cory. "They're mine."

Chapter 27

THERE HAD TO be a reasonable explanation. There just had to be. And that was exactly what Siobhan was determined to find out when she pulled open the door to the gallery and walked inside. "Hello? Anyone here?"

The girls had followed her in, but they stayed a few steps behind her, clearly willing to have her back while allowing her to run the show.

"Be right out," a woman's voice called from the back room.

Siobhan let her gaze track over the room. Her paintings were all organized at the front; other artists' work filled the rest of the space. The stark white walls were the perfect backdrop to the colorful collection in front of her.

Her perusal was interrupted by a short woman with shoulder-length blond hair. She looked to be in her late twenties or early thirties. She approached with her hand outstretched. "Hi. Welcome to the Lost Diamond Gallery. My name is Liza. Can I help you?"

Siobhan woodenly shook Liza's hand. This didn't make any

sense. Siobhan didn't even know this woman. "Where did you get those paintings in the front?"

Liza's smile dimmed slightly, and Siobhan figured it was in response to her harsh tone. "I believe they came from the owner's private collection."

"You're not the owner?" Siobhan asked.

"No, I'm the interim curator overseeing the opening."

"Could you please tell me who *is* the owner?"

"Yes. His name is Mr. Derick Miller."

"Oh, my God." Siobhan heard the gasp from behind her.

Liza looked puzzled. "Do you know him?"

Siobhan took a deep breath in an effort to keep the tears that had begun to sting her eyes from falling. "No. I don't know him at all." She turned to leave but stopped with her hand pressed against the door. She turned back to look at Liza. "You said you're the interim curator, right? Who's the permanent one?"

Liza's eyes moved between the girls curiously. "A woman," she said, "named Siobhan. Miss Siobhan Dempsey."

Chapter 28

DERICK PACED ON the runway next to his jet, gripping his phone against his ear with white knuckles as he listened to the seemingly endless ringing. When the voice mail came on, he left a message. His sixth so far.

"Siobhan. It's me again. I'm starting to panic here. Please call back as soon as you can."

Derick lowered the phone and stared at the display, silently cursing himself for never bothering to get the phone numbers of the other girls.

Siobhan had said she'd meet him at three. It was almost three forty-five. Where the hell could she be?

Helplessness was not a feeling Derick was fond of. He was never helpless. Feeling an irrational anger at Siobhan for putting him through this, he called her again.

This time, he heard the call connect, though Siobhan hadn't actually said anything yet.

Derick's words instantly filled the line. "Siobhan? Where are you? Are you okay?"

There was no immediate response, just the sound of her breathing on the other end.

"Is something wrong? Baby, are you okay?"

He heard her bitter laugh.

Derick was still worried, but now for a very different reason. "Please talk to me," he whispered.

"Talk to you? Why? What's left to say?" Her voice sounded like it was vibrating with anger but also wavering with sadness.

Derick's worry turned to all-out fear. It caused him to hesitate, and Siobhan filled in the silence.

"I thought we were past all this bullshit. But we'll never really be past it, will we, Derick?"

"Siobhan, I don't know what's wrong, but why don't you meet me at the airport, and then we can—"

"I'm not coming to the airport. It's done. We're done. Forever this time."

The call ended, and all Derick could do was stare out over the tarmac and wonder how this had happened all over again.

Curious to see how it all ends?

"PLEASE DON'T LET ME FALL."

Since Siobhan has made it as an artist, she's ready for a fresh start in New York with the love of her life, billionaire Derick Miller. But their relationship has been a roller-coaster ride that has pushed Derick too far. Will Siobhan be able to win back her soul mate?

Read on for a sneak peek at the final book in the Diamond Trilogy, *Exquisite,* available only from

DERICK STARED AT the piece of cardstock in his hand and read it once more. It wasn't that he didn't *want* to see the words written on it; it was just that he couldn't bring himself to fully believe them.

Not only did he receive an invitation to the Lost Diamond's grand opening that would be taking place next week, Siobhan had been the one to invite him. He hadn't even known she was back in New York, let alone planning to run the gallery.

There hadn't been any calls between them since he'd spoken to her about the deed. No texts or emails had been exchanged. He'd been sure that she didn't want to see him. And yet, the invitation in his hand proved differently.

But he wasn't exactly sure he wanted to see her.

Derick breathed heavily and then tossed the invitation on his counter before grabbing his coat and heading downstairs. He needed to go for a walk to clear his head.

The cool, crisp air hit him in the face as he exited the building. It was exactly what he needed. Maybe the sounds and sights of the city would be enough to get his mind off her. He rubbed his hands together and blew into them before thrusting them into his pockets and heading down the street.

The movement soothed him, so he walked quickly, crossing streets and turning down others. He'd covered two miles before he'd even realized where he was.

Somehow, in his effort to get away from thoughts of Siobhan and the gallery, he'd ended up right in front of it. His feet had taken him where his mind didn't want to go.

Stopping across the street from the gallery, he looked into the glass exterior, hoping to catch a glimpse of her. Maybe this was best. It didn't matter that they weren't together anymore, that they wouldn't be together. He needed to make sure she was okay, happy. He knew attending the opening was unlikely. What would he even say? Congratulations on the gallery I bought for you?

Yup. Voyeurism was definitely way less awkward.

He could see a woman on the phone writing something down, but there was no sign of Siobhan in there. He watched for another few minutes before deciding that he should go home. He took in a deep breath, letting the cool air hit the back of his throat.

And that's when he saw her.

She cautiously emerged from the back of the gallery, her slender fingers wrapped around a painting. She spoke to the other woman for a moment before moving toward the front of the gallery to position the art on an easel in the window display.

Then she pointed toward the side wall and said something else before grabbing some nearby boxes and heading toward the back of the gallery again. She looked so graceful, so confident, so self-assured.

This was where she was supposed to be. Even if he wasn't there with her.

Will you marry me for $10,000,000?

Read on for an extract

IT WAS A Friday morning and Janey Ellis was running late. As usual. She prided herself on being so low maintenance that she could make it from bed to car in twelve minutes flat. The only problem was the getting-out-of-bed part. This morning she could barely drag herself to the shower, having spent the previous evening reading scripts until midnight. Flowerpot Studios had three new TV shows going to series this season, and she was expected to give notes on all of them today—*if* she made it to work in time for her first call.

Sebastian, her ex, used to call her a lane-change demon, and it was true: she would never let some boring gray Prius slow her down. Indeed, she was weaving west on Sunset so fast she would have missed the billboard if it hadn't usurped the one for *her* show. The bright-yellow ad was wrapped around one whole side of a fifteen-story building that until yesterday had promoted the cop drama *Loyal Blue*. *Loyal Blue* was the only successful TV show that Janey had developed to date—the one that looked like it was going to secure her job for the next few years. But it had been cancelled. The finale had aired.

It wasn't her fault. Shows got cancelled all the time, and shows ran for years with worse ratings than *Loyal Blue*. It was a crapshoot. Nonetheless, as Janey's boss had put it, "Money is money and failure is failure." The towering building that had once showcased her success now displayed two-foot-tall Crayola-green letters reading: WILL YOU MARRY ME FOR $10,000,000?

The message was so bold and unexpected that it distracted Janey from wallowing in the sad fate of *Loyal Blue*. This was quite a departure from the TV ads that rotated through this prime Hollywood ad real estate. Janey slowed to gawk. It had to be another reality dating show, right? She cursed herself for not having been the one to come up with it. But then she read the rest of the sign: CREATIVE, OPEN-MINDED BUSINESSMAN WITH LIMITED TIME AND DESIRE TO PLAY THE FIELD. THIS IS A SERIOUS PROPOSAL.

Janey chuckled to herself. It was just weird enough to be legit. Dude obviously had some cash—she'd seen the budget line for the lease on that billboard, and it wasn't cheap. Cars started to honk, and Janey realized the light in front of her was green. She hit the gas a bit harder than she meant to and hurtled through the intersection.

The billboard vanished from Janey's mind as she dashed across the studio lot and hurried into the Flowerpot offices, but not for long. Inside she was a bit surprised to see that everyone—executives and assistants alike—was gathered in her boss's office. Uh-oh. This couldn't be good. After dropping her bag in her office, Janey went to see what was going on.

The roomful of people was staring out the window. "You can see the back of the building, over to the right," an assistant was saying.

"Check out the gridlock," someone else said.

"What's going on?" Janey whispered to her assistant, Elody.

"It's an ad," Elody said. "A ten-million-dollar marriage proposal. It went up this morning and has already gone viral. Gawker says it's caused three fender benders so far."

"I saw it on my way in," Janey said, feeling briefly proud that, for once, she hadn't been the one in the fender bender. "It's got to be some kind of hoax."

"Or a publicity stunt," her colleague Marco said. "Some wannabe actor decided to go big or go home."

"I think it's romantic," Elody said.

A voice boomed over the rest of them. "It's a waste of time and money. This isn't a watercooler, people. It's my office. Out."

Inwardly Janey kicked herself at her mistake. Her boss, J. Ferris White, had been known to can people for taking lunch breaks. Not long lunch breaks. Any lunch break at all. And after the collapse of *Loyal Blue* she needed to get back on his good side. She ducked out of the office with everyone else, feeling twelve years old.

AT 11:00 A.M. on the dot Suze Lee allowed herself her first coffee break of the day. Redfield Partners, though a small venture capital group based in LA, prided itself on offering all the benefits of a big Silicon Valley tech company. Pool and Ping-Pong tables, a half court for basketball, a fully stocked kitchen. The free coffee was supposed to stimulate them to work longer and later, but Suze was pretty sure the excuse for frequent breaks had cut her colleagues' productivity in half. She therefore limited herself to two visits to the café every day, twenty minutes each. Just coffee, no snacking. Today something was different. The café was strangely quiet. The persistent ping-pong of the game that never seemed to cease was silent for once. Instead there was a cluster of people around one of the café tables, where Kevin sat with his laptop.

"I'm sure the guy is sixty years old and ugly as a dog, looking for arm candy," Emily said.

"No! People in the comments are saying that he's a tech billionaire. Too busy to waste time dating," Kevin said. "I mean, for all we know, he's upstairs now, watching the Tweets roll in." The second floor of Redfield Partners was home to the executive suites, where the investing and operations teams of the firm had their offices (open concept, of course, but still a floor above everyone else). There they met with eager start-ups, counted their millions, and worked out daily in the on-site gym. It was easy to fit it all in when you knew you were set for life. Suze, Kevin, the ten other "entrepreneurs in residence," and the support staff were always encouraged to use the gym, but none of them ever did. Who wanted the hyperfit, life-balance-obsessed partners to see them panting on a treadmill at a slow jog? Instead they took ownership of the in-house café, some of them subsisting solely on its PowerBars and caffeinated beverages.

"Suze—you should totally apply," Meredith said.

Suze practically spat out her iced coffee. "What are you talking about? Why me?"

"Don't play dumb," Meredith said. "I have walked down the street with you. Every man we pass drools, and those are the ones who don't even know that you're brilliant."

"And you're nice. Mostly. A little uptight, but in a nice way," Kevin chimed in.

"Thanks?" said Suze.

"You're the hottest catch in LA," said Jeff.

There was an awkward silence. Jeff, the office IT guy, rarely spoke. When he did, it was always a little creepy.

"He's right," Meredith finally said. "A ten-million-dollar catch."

Suze rolled her eyes. "If that were true…wouldn't I have been caught by now?"

"For ten million dollars you might as well find out," said Kevin.

JAMES PATTERSON

BOOK**SHOTS**

OUT THIS MONTH

THE CHRISTMAS MYSTERY

Two priceless paintings disappear from a Park Avenue
murder scene – French detective Luc Moncrief is in
for a not-so-merry Christmas.

COME AND GET US

Miranda Cooper's life takes a terrifying turn when an SUV deliberately
runs her and her husband off a desolate Arizona road.

RADIANT: THE DIAMOND
TRILOGY, PART 2

Siobhan has moved to Detroit following her traumatic break-up
with Derick, but when Derick comes after her, Siobhan
must decide whether she can trust him again . . .

HOT WINTER NIGHTS

Allie Fairchild made a mistake when she moved to Montana,
but just when she's about to throw in the towel, life in
Bear Mountain takes a surprisingly sexy turn . . .

JAMES
PATTERSON
BOOKSHOTS
COMING SOON

HIDDEN

Rejected by the Navy SEALs, Mitchum is content to be his small town's unofficial private eye, until his beloved 14-year-old cousin is abducted. Now he'll call on every lethal skill to track her down . . .

THE HOUSE HUSBAND

Detective Teaghan Beaumont is getting closer and closer to discovering the truth about Darien Marshall. But there's a twist that she – and you, dear reader – will never see coming.

EXQUISITE: THE DIAMOND TRILOGY, PART 3

Siobhan and Derick's relationship has been a rollercoaster ride that has pushed Derick too far. Will Siobhan be able to win back her soul mate?

KISSES AT MIDNIGHT

Three exciting romances – *The McCullagh Inn in Maine*, *Sacking the Quarterback* and *Seducing Shakespeare*.

SEDUCING SHAKESPEARE (ebook only)

William Shakespeare has fallen in love – with the beautiful Marietta DiSonna. But what Shakespeare doesn't know is that Marietta is acting a role. Unless Shakespeare can seduce her in return . . .

ALSO BY JAMES PATTERSON

ALEX CROSS NOVELS
Along Came a Spider
Kiss the Girls
Jack and Jill
Cat and Mouse
Pop Goes the Weasel
Roses are Red
Violets are Blue
Four Blind Mice
The Big Bad Wolf
London Bridges
Mary, Mary
Cross
Double Cross
Cross Country
Alex Cross's Trial (*with Richard DiLallo*)
I, Alex Cross
Cross Fire
Kill Alex Cross
Merry Christmas, Alex Cross
Alex Cross, Run
Cross My Heart
Hope to Die
Cross Justice
Cross the Line

THE WOMEN'S MURDER CLUB SERIES
1st to Die
2nd Chance (*with Andrew Gross*)
3rd Degree (*with Andrew Gross*)
4th of July (*with Maxine Paetro*)
The 5th Horseman (*with Maxine Paetro*)

The 6th Target (*with Maxine Paetro*)
7th Heaven (*with Maxine Paetro*)
8th Confession (*with Maxine Paetro*)
9th Judgement (*with Maxine Paetro*)
10th Anniversary (*with Maxine Paetro*)
11th Hour (*with Maxine Paetro*)
12th of Never (*with Maxine Paetro*)
Unlucky 13 (*with Maxine Paetro*)
14th Deadly Sin (*with Maxine Paetro*)
15th Affair (*with Maxine Paetro*)

DETECTIVE MICHAEL BENNETT SERIES
Step on a Crack (*with Michael Ledwidge*)
Run for Your Life (*with Michael Ledwidge*)
Worst Case (*with Michael Ledwidge*)
Tick Tock (*with Michael Ledwidge*)
I, Michael Bennett (*with Michael Ledwidge*)
Gone (*with Michael Ledwidge*)
Burn (*with Michael Ledwidge*)
Alert (*with Michael Ledwidge*)
Bullseye (*with Michael Ledwidge*)

PRIVATE NOVELS
Private (*with Maxine Paetro*)
Private London (*with Mark Pearson*)
Private Games (*with Mark Sullivan*)
Private: No. 1 Suspect (*with Maxine Paetro*)
Private Berlin (*with Mark Sullivan*)

Private Down Under (*with Michael White*)

Private L.A. (*with Mark Sullivan*)

Private India (*with Ashwin Sanghi*)

Private Vegas (*with Maxine Paetro*)

Private Sydney (*with Kathryn Fox*)

Private Paris (*with Mark Sullivan*)

The Games (*with Mark Sullivan*)

NYPD RED SERIES

NYPD Red (*with Marshall Karp*)

NYPD Red 2 (*with Marshall Karp*)

NYPD Red 3 (*with Marshall Karp*)

NYPD Red 4 (*with Marshall Karp*)

STAND-ALONE THRILLERS

Sail (*with Howard Roughan*)

Swimsuit (*with Maxine Paetro*)

Don't Blink (*with Howard Roughan*)

Postcard Killers (*with Liza Marklund*)

Toys (*with Neil McMahon*)

Now You See Her (*with Michael Ledwidge*)

Kill Me If You Can (*with Marshall Karp*)

Guilty Wives (*with David Ellis*)

Zoo (*with Michael Ledwidge*)

Second Honeymoon (*with Howard Roughan*)

Mistress (*with David Ellis*)

Invisible (*with David Ellis*)

The Thomas Berryman Number

Truth or Die (*with Howard Roughan*)

Murder House (*with David Ellis*)

Never Never (*with Candice Fox*)

Woman of God (*with Maxine Paetro*)

BOOKSHOTS

Black & Blue (*with Candice Fox*)

Break Point (*with Lee Stone*)

Cross Kill

Private Royals (*with Rees Jones*)

The Hostage (*with Robert Gold*)

Zoo 2 (*with Max DiLallo*)

Heist (*with Rees Jones*)

Hunted (*with Andrew Holmes*)

Airport: Code Red (*with Michael White*)

The Trial (*with Maxine Paetro*)

Little Black Dress (*with Emily Raymond*)

Chase (*with Michael Ledwidge*)

Let's Play Make-Believe (*with James O. Born*)

Dead Heat (*with Lee Stone*)

Triple Threat

113 Minutes (*with Max DiLallo*)

The Verdict (*with Robert Gold*)

French Kiss (*with Richard DiLallo*)

$10,000,000 Marriage Proposal (*with Hilary Liftin*)

Kill or Be Killed

Taking the Titanic (*with Scott Slaven*)

Killer Chef (*with Jeffrey J. Keyes*)